Hard Stone

When range detective Rance Dehner kills outlaw Tully Brooks, he finds that the case will not be closed so easily. Before dying, Brooks tells Dehner that he was involved in a fake bank robbery in which no money was stolen. An innocent man has been arrested for the hold up, and Brooks wants Dehner to investigate.

Dehner's compliance with a dying man's request sends him to Hard Stone, Colorado, where the fake robbery took place. This prosperous mining town is layered in mystery and violence; Dehner must deal with a high-stakes gambler, a mining engineer who's always quick to draw his gun, and a mysterious assailant who seems determined to ambush and kill the detective. With enemies all around him, can Dehner get to the bottom of this before it's too late?

Hard Stone

James Clay

A Black Horse Western
ROBERT HALE

© James Clay 2016
First published in Great Britain 2016

ISBN 978-0-7198-1939-1

The Crowood Press
The Stable Block
Crowood Lane
Ramsbury
Marlborough
Wiltshire SN8 2HR

www.crowood.com

Robert Hale is an imprint
of The Crowood Press

Printed and bound in Great Britain by
CPI Group (UK) Ltd, Croydon CR0 4YY

CHAPTER ONE

Tully Brooks crept along the back of the buildings in Hard Stone, Colorado. The hour was late and the only sounds were barking dogs and revelers at the town's three saloons.

Tully stopped at the bank. The back door was unlocked as had been previously arranged. Stepping inside, the gunman felt a strange nervousness. This job was like no other he had ever pulled.

From the small storage area where Tully had entered, he continued through an open door into the bank proper. The outlaw paused beside the short row of tellers' cages, then made his way toward a yellow light, which stood on the desk of George Conklin. As he approached the desk, Tully mused to himself that Conklin did not look like a typical banker. He was a stocky, muscular man somewhere in his thirties, with leathery skin. His appearance fit well in a town populated by miners.

Conklin looked up from his paperwork. 'Right on time, Mr Brooks. Wish I could do business with more men as conscientious as you.'

'From what I understand, you and I will never do business again.'

Conklin smiled, pulled out a cigar, then returned it to

his suit pocket, apparently deciding this occasion did not merit a smoke. 'That's right, Mr Brooks. After tonight, you are never to return to Hard Stone. Understand?'

Tully didn't reply.

Conklin decided to let it pass. He pulled out a drawer and tossed a small roll of bills onto his desk, followed by a brown canvas sack. 'Five hundred dollars, like I promised.'

Tully Brooks picked up the money and counted it.

'Don't you trust me, Mr Brooks?'

'No.'

Conklin laughed, but there was a nervous quiver in it. He grabbed a newspaper from the top of his desk, crumpled it up and placed it in the canvas bag. 'In case anyone sees you riding off.'

Out of habit, Tully gave the bank a once over. His eyes went first to the large safe standing a few feet behind Conklin. The outlaw noted with some amusement that for once, the safe held no importance for him. He noticed that the shade on the bank's one window was pulled down. Did Conklin do that all the time, or would it cause people to wonder? He let out an impatient breath and took the bag. 'Ready?'

'Not yet.' The banker bolted from his desk. He took a few quick strides to the window and peeked around the shade. 'Everything is set. We need to move fast.'

Taking his own advice, Conklin hurried back to the desk, opened the right-hand drawer, and took out a pistol. 'Start running.'

Brooks grabbed the canvas bag, pulled his bandanna over his nose and fled from the bank. He ran around the corner and mounted his strawberry roan. Loud steps sounded from the boardwalk in front of the bank. George

Conklin shouted, 'The bank is being robbed!'

Tully galloped off as the banker fired at him. The shot came close. An angry Tully Brooks considered returning fire and killing the snake, but that didn't seem right. This was, after all, easy money.

CHAPTER TWO

Red splattered across the sky like blood on a battlefield. Rance Dehner crouched in a maze of bushes on a small knoll and contemplated the irony of sunrise. Poets rhapsodized over the beauty of dawn; for the detective, dawn was the time when he often caught up with and arrested a fugitive. Or killed him.

Dehner hoped this morning's confrontation would end in an arrest. Two previous encounters with Tully Brooks had involved gunplay and both had ended with Brooks getting away. But the detective had gained a respect for his opponent, who was one of the wiliest crooks he had ever chased.

Dehner had to devise a plan quickly. Tully was breaking camp. The outlaw had just saddled his horse and seemed to be checking his work to make sure the saddle was secure.

In one sudden movement, Tully ripped his rifle from its boot and fired in the direction of the detective. 'Good morning, friend,' Tully yelled as he levered the Henry. 'You're too late for breakfast!' He fired again.

Dehner rolled as shots ricocheted around him. On his stomach, he yelled, 'You're a lousy cook anyhow, Tully!'

'Rance?!' the outlaw yelled back.

'Yep.'

'You're one stubborn cuss!' The outlaw ran to the other side of his horse, using the animal as a shield. He knew his opponent well: Rance wouldn't shoot the animal.

'You're right, Tully. I'm a stubborn cuss. If I was a gentleman, I'd have a better job than this one! Give up, Tully!'

'You know I won't!' Brooks slipped the Henry back into the boot. 'Let's take a morning ride!' Tully quickly mounted the roan, spurring his steed into a fast gallop.

Dehner ran down the knoll to where his bay was tethered. He rode the horse cautiously up the small hill and then down the slope. Once they were on flat ground, Dehner raked his spurs against the horse and began a fast pursuit.

Two ribbons of dust trailed behind Tully's horse. Dehner kept his bay at a fast, steady gallop. Tully was pushing his horse hard, riding toward a mountain where he hoped to get lost among the caves and large rocks.

The outlaw had reached the foot of the mountain when his roan stumbled and fell. Tully was thrown off the animal but quickly made it back onto his feet. Checking the fallen horse, he saw that his Henry was underneath the animal. He glanced back. Rance was fast approaching. Tully gave up on retrieving the rifle. He began to hobble up the mountain.

Rance reined in near the injured horse. He dismounted and took a quick look at the roan. The animal was blowing hard and seemed to be in terrible pain. The detective spotted Tully's Henry under the horse, but there was no time to check further on the roan. The detective tethered his own horse with a heavy stone and pulled his Winchester from the boot.

He moved away from the bay and ran behind a boulder near the foot of the mountain, where he shouted,

'Surrender, Tully! For once in your life, act smart!'

There was no response. Dehner wasn't expecting one. The detective thought it significant that Tully Brooks hadn't fired at him. Tully didn't have his rifle and the outlaw was apparently in a position where a pistol shot was unlikely to hit its target, and would only expose the shooter's location.

Going after an injured Tully Brooks was like going after an injured bear, Rance thought to himself. 'Guess I'm paid to be a hunter,' he whispered as he started up the mountain.

The mountainside was a jigsaw of scattered boulders and clumps of thin trees. Dehner zigzagged his way up the steep slope, occasionally taking refuge behind a large rock. He didn't want to make himself an easy target.

He was scanning the mountainside from behind a boulder when he heard gravel scattering above him. The detective turned to spot the blur of a terrifying force charging at him. The sound of Rance's rifle fire blended with the mountain lion's roar. The lion twisted backwards, and then straightened for another attack. Rance levered another shell into the chamber of the Winchester. His second shot brought the cat down.

The detective breathed heavily as he approached the beast, which was defeated but still alive. A third shot killed the mountain lion.

Dehner felt hard iron pressing into his back. 'Good shootin', Rance. I always admired the way you could handle a gun. Now, toss the rifle and put your hands up.'

Rance did what he was told. He kept his hands very high. Brooks had the barrel of a pistol pressed into his back and didn't seem too concerned about the Colt. 45 tied to his right leg. Dehner wanted to prolong the indifference. He spoke in a casual, friendly manner. 'You're a hard man to spot, Tully. Where were you hiding?'

'In those trees behind the rocks.' He gave a light-hearted chuckle, 'I spotted the cat, but the cat didn't see me. No, she had her eyes on you the moment you started up the mountain. I thought I'd hang back and enjoy the fight.'

'Sorry to disappoint you with the outcome.'

'A man must always fight to win.' Regret edged Tully's voice. 'Sorry, Rance, gotta—'

The detective arced his back and smashed his head into Tully's face. The outlaw's arms splayed out and his pistol fired. Dehner felt the heat from the shot as his entire body collided with Tully Brooks.

Both men plunged to the ground and skidded down the slope. Dehner palmed his Colt and smoked a shot into Tully's chest seconds before the outlaw collided with the boulder Dehner had been crouched behind.

Tully Brooks dropped his gun; a second explosion from Dehner's pistol landed near the fallen weapon. A needless precaution: Tully was using the boulder to lift himself up but his hopes of retrieving the weapon were a foolish dream. The detective hurried to his feet and grabbed Brooks's Smith & Wesson. 'You won't be needing this anymore, Tully.'

''Fraid you're right.' The outlaw leaned his upper torso against the rock, then closed his eyes and slid to the ground.

CHAPTER THREE

Tully Brooks opened his eyes and thought he was in hell. Bright flames dominated his vision, and a terrible pain twisted through his body. But the cup handed to him made him reconsider.

'Guess they don't serve coffee in hell,' Brooks spoke as he slowly sat up, accepted the cup, and leaned against the tree that was behind him.

'If they do, it probably tastes like mine,' Rance Dehner said.

Tully took a sip. 'It might at that.'

'Getting you off that mountain was no easy job.' Dehner looked back at the mountain as he sipped from his own cup. 'Your wound is serious. Tomorrow morning I'll ride into Hard Stone and bring back a doctor.'

'What about Grinder?'

'Who?'

'My horse, Grinder, I know he took a bad fall....'

The anxious quality in Tully's voice caused Dehner to speak softly. 'He had a broken leg. I'm sorry.'

Brooks looked away for a moment. 'You know, Grinder was a little past his prime, shoulda got me a new horse. But ... he was the only friend I had. Just couldn't give him up.'

The detective allowed his prisoner a few moments of silence. He realized that Brooks needed a diversion and provided it with a question. 'You seemed to be riding toward Hard Stone. Why?'

Tully laughed carefully. He was in too much pain not to be cautious. 'Funny ... I've lived a pretty useless life ... the one time I decide to do somethin' decent, I end up gettin' shot.'

Dehner remained on his feet and looked at Tully curiously. If the prisoner wanted to talk, Dehner would listen.

'How did you happen on my trail, Rance? I mean, who hired that detective agency you work for to get me?'

'The Lowrie Agency has what you might call a standing order on you.'

Once again, Tully laughed softly. 'Bet it's from Wells Fargo—those hold-ups I pulled last year.'

Dehner nodded his head. 'I was finishing up a case in Denver when I got word you had been there. Decided to look into it. You've made a fool out of me in the past, Tully. Guess I got sort of a bur under my saddle about capturing you.'

'I was the fool in Denver, just went there to have a good time. Made one big mistake.'

'What was that?'

'Read a newspaper.' Tully Brooks paused for several moments. He tried to look calm but his body trembled. The outlaw seemed to be battling a terrible wave of pain.

The wave passed, or at least subsided. 'Tell me, Rance, hear anything about a bank hold-up in Hard Stone about two weeks ago?'

'Can't say I have.'

'That was my last job; helped a banker rob his own bank.'

Brooks enjoyed the surprised expression on Dehner's face. He explained about his experience in Hard Stone.

'Sounds crazy.' Dehner stared into the fire as if an answer might be there. He looked back at Tully Brooks. 'You said there was something in a Denver paper about all this?'

'That's why I was ridin' back to Hard Stone.' Tully took a long sip of coffee and waited for it to settle. 'The paper says they arrested a man for pullin' that robbery. Accordin' to the *Rocky Mountain News*, a jasper named Slushy Snow saw the robber ride off and has identified the thief. They got him in jail.'

'Slushy Snow?' Dehner barked a laugh. 'What's the name

of the man they've jailed?'

'Can't remember, nothin' special 'bout the name that'd make it stick in your mind. But I know this: Slushy Snow is lyin'.'

'Sounds like there was more to your last job than you thought.' Dehner gave his prisoner a cock-eyed expression. 'Don't tell me you were going back to Hard Stone to confess to the crime!'

'Don't know exactly. I sure don't want an innocent man gettin' framed for somethin' I done.' Tully raised the cup of java to his lips, this time taking only a small sip. He seemed to be using the gesture to collect his thoughts. 'Know why I became an outlaw, Rance?'

Dehner shook his head.

Tully answered his own question. 'Boredom. Laziness. Never cared much for workin' steady. Thought bein' an outlaw would be excitin' and fun. I was just gonna do it for a year or so, but it didn't work out that way. I also thought I'd never kill anyone....'

'That didn't work out either, did it?'

'No.' This time Tully only stared at his coffee. 'I'm thirty-eight years old. With Grinder gone, I got no friends. I never had a home. I gotta pay anytime I want to keep company with a female. Maybe I thought goin' back to Hard Stone would make up for some things.'

Brooks looked in the direction of the mining town. His eyes conveyed the deep sadness of opportunity delayed too long. 'You and me got certain things in common, Rance.'

'Like what?'

'We're in the same line of work, just on different sides. Both of us are always careful about not leavin' much of a trail. Good idea, I suppose. But in the end, you're a man who just disappears one day and nobody much cares.'

Dehner once again peered into the fire, this time to avoid having to reply to his prisoner. When he looked back, Tully Brooks had set down his coffee. His arms were crossed and pressing against his body.

'I got a favor to ask, Rance.'

'Go ahead.'

'I'm not gonna be up to doin' much for a while. Could you ride into Hard Stone? Don't want an innocent man to suffer....'

'Sure.'

'Thanks.'

Rance steadied the outlaw and helped him to lie back down. He then opened his own bedroll and tried to get some rest. Sleep didn't come easy. Dehner wondered if someday, down the trail, he would face a similar predicament to that of Tully.

The color of blood was again returning to the sky when Dehner awoke to cries of pain. He scrambled over to Tully Brooks, whose forehead was dotted with drops of perspiration. Rance tried to speak in a comforting voice. 'I'm going down to the stream and get you a cold, wet cloth.' He took off his bandanna. 'We'll bring down that fever. After that, I'll get the doc.'

'Yep ... thanks.'

Tully listened to Rance's departing footsteps and then began to cry. He cried for the marshal he had killed two years back. He wept for a life he had never lived, for friendships never made and for the girl he had loved when he was sixteen and whose name he couldn't remember.

Tully thought he heard Rance's footsteps hurrying back and tried to stop the tears; he couldn't let Rance see him bawling like a baby. That would be a terrible humiliation, he had to stop....

When the detective crouched over Tully Brooks, he knew the cold cloth would be of no use. He mistook the dampness on the outlaw's face for perspiration.

CHAPTER FOUR

The trip to Hard Stone had a grotesque start. Dehner had no choice but to wrap Tully Brooks's corpse in a blanket and lay it across his horse, in front of the saddlehorn. The detective was happy to spot a small ranch, a quarter mile or so into his journey. He stopped to buy a horse.

The owner of the ranch was a short overweight man named Ezra. He was obviously interested in Dehner's cargo but didn't mention it, as if to do so would be a discourtesy.

Rance bought a small buckskin. Ezra watched as he lifted Tully's body off of his bay and placed it onto his new purchase. The rancher offered no assistance but gave out some business advice.

'Ever been ta Hard Stone before?'

'No,' Dehner replied as he tied the corpse securely to the buckskin.

'When ya git there talk ta Rufus. He owns the livery. He'll buy that buckskin from ya, if you want, but ya gotta argua with him. You won't git a fair price lessen ya argua.'

'Obliged.' Dehner mounted his bay and continued his journey.

The detective reached Hard Stone later that morning. The town appeared busy and prosperous. Dehner observed that no one took much interest in a stranger riding down Main Street with a dead body strewn across his pack horse.

There was one exception to Dehner's observation. A man wearing a black suit with a string tie walked out into the middle of the street to greet the newcomer.

'Hello, stranger.'

Dehner stopped his horse and held out his right hand. 'The name is Rance Dehner.'

'Thorton Nevin. I'm the pastor of Faith Church, Hard Stone's finest church. That is not really boasting. Faith Church is the only church in Hard Stone.'

As he shook the pastor's hand, Rance was certain the clergyman used the finest church-only church line often when meeting strangers. Up close, Dehner also observed that Reverend Nevin's face was pock-marked and pinched. He surmised that the clergyman had been seriously ill, though the sickness probably went back several years. He pegged Nevin's age at about forty, though the pastor's health problems may have piled some time onto that guess.

'It looks like you have had a rough day, Mr Dehner.' Thorton Nevin pointed to the dead body on the buckskin.

Rance nodded his head and explained that he was a detective who had killed Tully Brooks, a man wanted for robbery and murder. 'I have a very unpleasant job ahead of me, Reverend.'

'Oh.'

'I need to get a picture of Brooks's corpse and send it back to my agency's headquarters in Dallas. That's the only way we can collect money from Wells Fargo, our client in this case.' Dehner paused for a moment as if embarrassed to continue. 'My boss prefers that the picture be of the corpse lying in a coffin. He believes that eliminates any doubt as to

16

whether the subject is really dead.'

Thorton Nevin laughed good-naturedly. 'Don't feel bad, Mr Dehner, I suppose this country was built by industry as well as charity.' He employed his head to gesture down the street. 'Take the body to Rimstead's Barber Shop. Henry Rimstead is both the town's undertaker and barber. I'll go get Will Bain. He runs the local newspaper and takes pictures on the side. He'll charge you—'

'That will be no problem.'

'Good.' The pastor looked up the street in the direction of the newspaper office. 'Will should be in right now, I'll—'

'One more thing, Reverend, I want Tully Brooks to have a Christian burial.'

The pastor looked surprised but smiled as he shrugged his shoulders. 'Sure. With this hot July weather, we'd best bury him today. We still have time. I can make arrangements.'

'I want him buried in a coffin, not just wrapped in an old blanket.'

'Well … yes … but that will cost—'

'I'll pay,' Dehner quickly replied.

Reverend Nevin's initial surprise was replaced by curiosity. 'You act as if this Tully Brooks was a friend of yours.'

Dehner remembered what Tully Brooks had told him less than twenty-four hours before: '… in the end, you're a man who just disappears one day and nobody much cares.'

'Yes, we were friends,' the detective said.

'And I will dwell in the house of the Lord forever. Amen.' Reverend Nevin closed his Bible and looked at Rance. 'Services like this are for the living, Mr Dehner. Are you sure there is nothing you want to say?'

Dehner looked at the hastily constructed wooden cross with Tully's name carved in it along with the year of his death. He thought about the strange bond that had developed between the hunter and the hunted.

'No thanks, Reverend. I have nothing to say.'

'Can I go now? I gotta fix them two shutters in the church.' The question came from a large man whose two hundred pounds draped a frame of slightly less than six feet. His eyes seemed to have a permanent look of confused anger.

'Yes, Tom, you may go. I appreciate you digging the grave for Mr Brooks.' After doing his work, Tom had remained at the grave for the service. His presence brought the attendance at Tully Brooks's funeral to three.

'Billy Collins hangs on them shutters every Sunday. That's how come they get loose.'

Thorton spoke in a quiet, pleasant voice. 'I know.'

Tom seemed offended by the pleasantness. 'You should make him stop doin' it. If his people don't make him stop, you gotta.'

'I'll do what I can. Thanks again for your help, Tom. I know Mr Dehner appreciates it too.'

Tom turned away abruptly as if he had just been insulted. The large man stomped toward the church and entered through the back door. Hard Stone's only cemetery was located behind Faith Church, which stood at the northern end of the town.

'Does Tom work for you, Reverend Nevin?'

'Well … yes. I can't pay much but I give him chores to do. That keeps him out of trouble, most of the time. Thank goodness Andy and Etta Fleming, who own a restaurant, attend church. They give Tom a free meal at noon.' The pastor gave a whimsical laugh. 'Andy reminds me every Sunday that Tom's meals are the family's contribution to the church.'

'Reverend Nevin, do you know anything about a bank hold-up that took place in Hard Stone—'

'Know anything!' Nevin seemed startled by the question, 'I seem to hear about nothing else! One of my parishioners, Lon Westlake, is in jail for the crime right now. His fiancée, Penelope Castle is devastated. I've tried to calm the girl, assure her that justice will be done when the circuit judge gets to town next week, but—'

'I can understand Westlake's fiancée thinking he's innocent. What about you, Reverend?'

'Oh yes, I believe he's innocent. Lon impresses me as a fine, honest man. I've known him for almost a year....'

The clergyman's voice trailed off. Something seemed to be bothering him.

'Any problems, Reverend?'

'I used to be an associate pastor at a large church in Denver. I ended up coming here when the man who founded this church died.'

'Yes?'

Reverend Nevin looked at the setting sun, then looked at the Bible in his right hand; neither seemed to give him much comfort. 'Most of the people who come West do so with the idea of starting a ranch or a farm or maybe even a company. They want to build something.'

Dehner nodded his head.

'A mining town is different. We aren't building anything here, just taking from the earth. People flood into a mining town from all over, hoping to make a fast dollar.'

'Miners are hard-working people,' Dehner said.

'Yes. But it's all so uncertain, so temporary. The mine could go on for years or be shut down tomorrow. And if the mine closed, so would the town. Within a few weeks, everyone would be gone.'

Reverend Thorton Nevin looked around him at the wooden crosses, 'Everyone except them.'

CHAPTER FIVE

After the graveside service, Dehner returned briefly to his hotel room where he had checked in earlier in the day, and spent some time reading back issues of the town's weekly newspaper. Within an hour of his arriving in Hard Stone, Will Bain had taken a picture of Tully Brooks's corpse lying in its coffin. Rance had accompanied the newspaper owner back to the clapboard structure which housed *The Hard Stone Sentinel* and purchased the two editions of the paper that had been published since the bank hold-up. He then checked into the town's only hotel and took a bath before attending the memorial service. Only after the service did he have time to give attention to the newspapers.

The edition published soon after the robbery quoted George Conklin as saying that the thief had caught him totally by surprise. 'He just suddenly appeared out of nowhere. I don't know how he got into the bank.'

The same edition contained a quote by Slushy Snow. 'That Lon Westlake is dumber than a mule. When he ran out the front door of the bank, his bandanna slipped down. The fool hadn't tied it right. Westlake was sure nervous. His hand was shaking and it took him a moment or two to yank it back up. I was right across the street.'

Dehner figured he needed to have a talk with both George Conklin and Slushy Snow.

The bank robbery continued to be the main story in the next edition of *The Hard Stone Sentinel*. Sheriff Pete Kendall was quoted as saying, 'Lon Westlake knows this town. He knows when the payroll for Castle Mining is sitting in the bank and that's when he struck. So far, the jasper won't tell anyone where he hid the cash.'

Harland Castle, who owned the mine, was more elevated in his remarks. 'The payroll was stolen but I have confidence it will be recovered soon. Castle Mining will pay a one thousand dollar reward to anyone who discovers the location of the money. Meanwhile, I take solace in the fact that our company was able to meet its payroll without that cash. We don't expect a single one of our hard-working employees to sacrifice a penny for this company. Our creditors have been patient with us, for which I will be eternally grateful. As many in this town know, we have recently discovered a new and very rich vein. No bad news should erase that fact from the minds of our good citizens. The future of Castle Mining and Hard Stone is very bright.'

The newspapers provided Rance with a decent start but no more. He left his room and headed for Fleming's Restaurant. He had been on the trail since leaving Denver and had eaten a lot of jerky. He enjoyed feasting on a dinner of steak, potatoes and corn on the cob, climaxed by apple pie. After the meal he walked briskly to the Lucky Miner Saloon where he hoped to get more information.

The moment he stepped up to the saloon's mahogany bar, Rance suspected that he, like Harlan Castle, had struck a rich vein. A cowboy, his face weathered and wrinkled from many hours in the sun, was leaning on the bar and making conversation with the bartender. Or trying to.

'… Glad I'm a cowhand, could never be a miner. I'll tell ya, it ain't natural spending your days in a hole. Hell, we're all gonna end up in the ground sooner or later, why hurry it?'

The bartender replied with an indifferent hum. He was young and well groomed, without a spot on his white shirt. Rance figured the barkeep also owned the saloon or at least was a part owner. The last thing the young man wanted to do was say something that could make the miners angry.

The cowboy sipped from the mug in front of him and continued, unaware of the barkeep's discomfort. 'I'll say this for minin', though, it sure makes a man hungry. Why, they can't bring in enough beef. There's a real need for a cattle ranch right here … even if it be a small one.'

The bartender spotted Dehner standing near the cowboy. 'What can I do for you, sir?'

Being called 'sir' by a bartender was a bit unusual. Rance ordered a beer. The bartender brought him his order, tossed the twenty-five cents Dehner gave him into a box under the bar and hurried off to serve other customers.

With the bartender at the opposite end of the bar, the cowboy addressed Rance. 'Never seen ya before.'

'Just arrived.' Rance introduced himself and shook hands with the cowhand, who gave his name as Buck Mitchell. The detective feigned interest as Buck expounded on a life 'workin' the grub line.' The stories weren't very interesting, which encouraged Dehner: Buck was a man who told the truth.

'Seems everyone in this town is jawing about the bank robbery a couple weeks ago,' Dehner spoke in a conversational manner.

The cowhand shrugged his shoulders in a gesture of contempt. 'I ain't got no money in a bank. Don't make no never mind to me.'

The detective wasn't ready to give up on Buck. 'From what I read in the paper, there was only one witness, a jasper with a really crazy name....' Rance crunched his face as if trying to give his memory a kick.

'Slushy Snow.' Buck once again sounded talkative. 'That one's a strange bird.'

The cowboy took a long drink from his mug and put it down empty. Dehner signaled the bartender to fill it back up. Buck nodded thanks as the detective tossed a coin onto the mahogany. Dehner maintained a casual voice as he once again faced his companion. 'This Slushy Snow, is he a friend of yours?'

'Na, but I met him once. I was roundin' up strays when my horse went lame. Ended up walkin' the chestnut ta an old prospector's cabin where Slushy lives now.'

'Sounds like Slushy Snow is a bit of a hermit.'

Mitchell shook his head. 'Na. The cabin is jus' a few miles west of the Lazy J; that's the outfit I works for. Three or four prospectors probably lived in that there cabin at one time. There's a corral in back and the cabin's plenty big. Na. Slushy ain't no hermit. He spends some time playin' cards, but he ain't exactly sociable.'

'What do you mean?'

'Well, when I got ta his place, he was helpful. Loaned me a horse; he has two in that corral. But he didn't ask me inside for a drink or nothin'.'

'Did you see him again?'

Buck busied himself with his second beer for a few

23

moments, and then continued. 'That chestnut of mine wasn't in too bad a fix, jus' needed to take it easy for a week or so. The next day I rode a horse belongin' to the Lazy J and returned Slushy's horse to him, only he weren't at home. I left the horse in the coral. Never talked to him again. I mean Slushy, not the horse!'

Buck laughed hard at his own joke. His guffaws were cut short by loud voices.

'You're cheatin', mister. You're nothin' but a dirty cheat!'

'Sir, a man's good name is his most precious possession. I must demand an immediate apology!'

'You damn crook, I'll never apologize to you!'

Dehner moved his head about to see where the trouble was coming from. The crowd had parted, giving the detective a clear view of a table now occupied by three men. A chair pushed back from the table indicated that there had been four until the argument broke out. Rance turned to Buck, who seemed to be enjoying the commotion. 'I'd know that voice anywhere—a friend of mine.'

'The guy who sounds like a limey?'

'Yep. His name's Stacey Hooper.'

'Ya ain't too particular about your friends. That guy is a sharper. I can tell by his clothes.'

'How about the other two?'

'Keith Amber, the guy accusin' Fancy Dan of bein' a cheat, has a real temper, but he dang near never draws a gun. The man sittin' across from him is Slade Pierson, a gunslick. Or he wants to be.'

'Thanks for the conversation, Buck.'

All the patrons of the Lucky Miner were now watching the drama being played out at the poker table. Most were keeping a safe distance, but Dehner took a few steps closer to the action. He had to back up Stacey Hooper. The detective mused to himself that his profession did indeed lead to odd friendships.

Stacey Hooper was adorned in a lavish gray frock coat with black bordering at the end of the sleeves, nicely complimented by his large silver cufflinks. He had black hair, green eyes, and a face that always appeared amused, even when he was in a dispute, as the gambler was now.

'That's quite enough, Mr Amber. Out of respect for the rest of your family, who I am sure are decent, God-fearing people, I have refrained from making a public spectacle of the fact that you are guilty of the very offense with which you have charged me.'

'Is that so? Prove it, sharper!' Amber was a large man with a pale complexion from too much time spent inside mines and inside saloons. He was carrying a gun. Slade Pierson's gun was in his hand and pointed under the table at Stacey Hooper. No gun was visible on Hooper's body but Dehner was certain it was there. Still, Stacey Hooper spent most of his time in cities. He might not be savvy to the tricks that accompany small-town hospitality.

Hooper looked around the saloon and smiled benignly, then addressed his accuser. 'I shall proceed to roll up my sleeves, if you promise to do the same.'

Amber hesitated. His eyes shot across the table. 'Sure. Why, Slade will tell ya, I'm as honest as they come. Ain't that right, Slade? Now, Mr Gambler, you just watch.'

Dehner palmed his Colt and pressed it into the back of Slade's neck. 'Holster that gun you're holding, friend. You're singing an old song and I don't want to hear it.'

'Sure, stranger.' Whiskey slurred Pierson's words.

The detective was ready as Slade turned to fire. Dehner

slammed his Colt against the gunslick's head. Pierson yelled in pain and hit the floor, face first. Rance quickly retrieved the gun his victim had dropped, then looked up and saw Stacey Hooper on his feet with a pistol in hand.

'Gentlemen, this unfortunate incident has left us too distracted to continue. Depart, Mr Amber, and take your over-zealous friend with you.' Stacey nodded toward the groaning figure on the floor. 'But tomorrow is another day. If you wish to win back your losses, I shall be here and happy to oblige.'

The gambler put away his gun and scooped the money from the table as Keith Amber helped Slade to his feet. Dehner emptied the cartridges from Pierson's gun and handed it to Amber. Keith Amber and the gunslick left, muttering low curses. Dehner didn't holster his gun until they were gone.

'You're getting a bit careless, Stacey,' Rance said.

'Please elaborate,' the gambler replied. 'You know how highly I value the insights of the West's finest detective.'

'Travelling gamblers are a target in a small town like Hard Stone,' Rance explained, as the saloon patrons returned to their fun. 'If a well-dressed dude cleans them out, one man threatens a fight. While the gambler is preoccupied with the guy who's yelling, another man puts a bullet in him. That way they get their money back and have a good story to talk about the next day.'

'And no one cares about the fate of the itinerant gambler.' Hooper shook his head. 'Plato was right. The masses well deserve the designation of "beast".'

A broad smile swept across Stacey Hooper's face. 'But why dwell on life's little shortcomings? You just saved my life, good friend.' Stacey motioned to the bartender, 'Bring us a bottle of your finest whiskey, please!'

Rance immediately noticed that his friend had simply ordered the whiskey; he had not mentioned paying for it. Dehner smiled inwardly. Stacey Hooper hadn't changed one bit.

CHAPTER SIX

The figure moved cautiously across the roof of Ray's Gunshop. So far, luck was on his side. No desk clerk had been around when he entered the hotel and saw the name of the man he needed to kill in the register. A quick check of the Lucky Miner revealed that his prey was spending some time in the saloon.

'He'll come back here tonight, I just gotta be patient,' the shooter whispered to himself.

His location was good. The gun shop stood directly across from the hotel and was two stories high. The roof was far above the occasional lanterns that splattered dabs of murky light along Main Street. A rope was now tied to the back of the building and a horse was ready for a quick escape.

He gripped his Winchester tighter as he heard a voice coming from up the street. 'Of course I was cheating, Rance. So was everyone else in the game, or they were trying to. Why, not to cheat at cards amounts to gambling, which is a sin.'

The killer saw two shadows advancing through the puddles of light. He couldn't take a chance on his target's friend coming after him. He would have to kill both men.

Hooper continued to pontificate as the two men approached the spot of light provided by one of the hotel's porch lamps. As they began to enter the light, a woman called out and rushed toward them. She seemed to have come from the general store beside the gun shop.

The woman was young and attractive. She joined Dehner and Hooper in front of the hotel. The shooter cursed inwardly; killing two strangers was one thing, no one would care, but killing a woman who was apparently a citizen of the town, and a very pretty woman to boot, would create pandemonium. He couldn't take a chance on missing his targets and shooting the woman; a posse would quickly be on his heels.

The killer tried to calm the anger burning inside him. He would have another chance soon.

Penelope Castle leaned against the counter of Westlake's General Store and counted her money. The young woman didn't know if she had enough. She had never hired a detective before.

Penelope had often been one of the last people to leave Westlake's General Store. Not an unusual situation for someone who was a bookkeeper as well as a clerk.

She brushed back her long reddish-brown hair and reflected on happier times, like the day she had stood nervously in front of Lon Westlake making her pitch for a job. 'I may not be a formally trained bookkeeper, Mr Westlake, but I have a head for figures. You can ask Mrs Stanfield. She will tell you I was the best student at arithmetic she ever had!'

Lon Westlake had hired her. Six months later he asked her to marry him. What followed seemed like magic. She cherished the memories of the one hour they had together in the store each day after Ralph Morris, the full-time clerk, had departed. Not that anything untoward happened! They kept the shades of the store wide open, not giving the gossips anything to chew on.

But she and Lon made silly jokes and talked about their future together as she worked on the books and Lon got the store ready for the next day. Then came that awful morning when she arrived at the store to find it still locked. A passing barfly had told her, 'If you're lookin' for Lon Westlake, missy, you'll find him in jail. He bein' the one who robbed the bank last night.'

Now, Penelope's eyes had been fixed on the store's front window. Seeing the men she had been watching for, the woman hurried out the front door and into the street.

'Excuse me, gentlemen!'

Dehner and Hooper halted near the splash of light in front of the hotel and turned to greet the young woman who stopped in front of them, looking very self-conscious. 'I know it is late, gentlemen, I'm sorry for being so rude.'

Stacey Hooper's smile was more lecherous than gracious. 'No apology is needed! An evening spent with ruffians is rarely concluded with the arrival of someone as lovely as yourself.'

To Stacey's disappointment, Penelope addressed Dehner. 'Sir, I understand you are a detective.'

Rance cringed, remembering how Stacey had called him 'the West's greatest detective' back in the saloon. 'Yes, my name is Rance Dehner.'

The woman noted the chagrin on Dehner's face. 'This is a small town, Mr Dehner.' She nodded at the store behind her. 'One of our regular customers witnessed the mishap at the Lucky Miner this evening. Knowing about my present circumstances, he came by and described you and your, ah, friend to me. I figured you'd be staying at the hotel....'

Penelope's voice trailed off. She inhaled before speaking again. 'Mr Dehner, I wish to hire you!'

The next fifteen minutes were spent with Dehner at first trying to put Penelope at ease, and then musing over the fact that her wishes were identical to those of Tully Brooks. She wanted Rance to find out who had really robbed the bank. The detective stopped Penelope when she began to approach the matter of money. 'I'm sure we can work out the fee at a later time, Miss Castle. I'll do what I can to help, but have you discussed this matter with the local law?'

Penelope nodded her head. 'Our sheriff, Pete Kendall, is a good man ... I suppose. But he has let the words of one witness close his mind. The bank was robbed on a very dark night, there was no moon—'

Dehner interrupted the young woman's case for the defense. 'I'll talk to Lon tomorrow. Can you come with me? He is likely to trust a stranger more if you introduce us.'

Impatience filled Penelope's face as she pointed across the street. 'I have things that must get done in the store tomorrow morning. I wish I didn't but ... could we meet at the General Store at, say, two in the afternoon? From there we can go to the jail.'

'Fine.' The detective paused, realizing the hour was late. 'Meanwhile, allow me to walk you home.'

'That's very kind of you. Thanks.'

'Propriety demands that I wish both of you good night, despite the fact that you both are oblivious to my presence!' Stacey Hooper turned and marched into the hotel.

'Oh dear!' Penelope put a hand to her cheek.

'Don't worry about my friend. He's temperamental, but harmless.'

Rance felt uneasy. He hated telling lies, even white lies. Stacey Hooper was anything but harmless.

CHAPTER SEVEN

Rance Dehner knocked on the door of Stacey Hooper's hotel room. The 'Come in' he received was laced with irritation.

The gambler stood in front of a pine bureau where an open whiskey flask had been placed beside the wash basin. Hooper rolled a cigarette as he glanced at his friend.

'Breakfast,' he said.

'I thought you smoked cigars,' Dehner replied.

'Cigars are for the evening. What time is it, anyway?'

'About seven in the morning,'

Stacey swished a match across the top of the bureau and set the flame to his handiwork. 'When the game is good, I'm usually turning in about now. How did things go with dear Penelope last night?'

'OK. I walked her home.'

'Is that all?'

'Yes!'

Stacey inhaled on his cigarette and let out a cloud of smoke. 'I swear, Rance, you must be descended from those wretched puritans that came over from England. The old country was happy to be rid of them—a bunch of pious sticks.'

'This afternoon I'm meeting with Lon Westlake. Penelope will be there along with her father, Harland—'

'Aha!' Hooper waved his right arm, scattering ashes in several directions. 'The truth emerges at last. When you arrived at the home of lovely Penelope, her father was waiting in the parlor and promptly drove off the bounder who wanted to soil his daughter's purity.'

'No. Her father was asleep. I'll meet him this afternoon. Penelope told me he usually accompanies her when she visits Lon in jail. Though, given the circumstances I'm sure he is not worried about his daughter's purity.'

Stacey shook his head and spoke in a melancholy voice. 'I always try to think of you in the very best manner, dear friend, and you always disappoint. Your afternoon itinerary is obviously full; what do you have planned for this morning?'

'I'm riding out to see Slushy Snow. He has a cabin just west of the Lazy J Ranch.' Dehner pointed downwards. 'My room is on the first floor. Before coming up I checked with the desk clerk and got directions to the ranch as well as to your room. Finding the cabin shouldn't be a problem.'

'I shall accompany you.'

That response surprised Dehner. 'I always took you for a city man, Stacey. How long do you plan to stay in Hard Stone?'

'Why, Rance, an innocent man's freedom is at stake. My humanitarian impulses demand that I remain here until justice is done. You do believe me, don't you?!'

'No. Come on, let's ride.'

Dehner's thoughts were on Stacey's very newly acquired spirit of civic responsibility. He didn't notice the man sitting in front of the hotel, his face hidden by a newspaper. Eyes peered around that paper and watched as Rance and his companion headed for the livery and their horses.

The figure slowly arose, left the paper on the chair, and followed far enough behind the two men that he wouldn't be spotted.

CHAPTER EIGHT

Dehner and Hooper tied up their horses at a hitch rail in front of Slushy Snow's cabin. 'Buck had it right,' the detective spoke in a whisper. 'This cabin is a bit off by itself but not really isolated. Not the cabin of a hermit.'

'And hermits aren't conscientious about appearances.'

Stacey had a point. The cabin had a fresh layer of white paint on it and the porch, which fronted the quarters, looked like a recent addition.

With Hooper behind him, Dehner stepped onto the porch and was about to knock on the door when he was stopped by a gunshot.

Both men turned around. Dehner's Colt .45 was in his hand as they faced a rider seated on a large gray. Smoke still trickled from the rider's gun, which had been fired into the air. A large hat shadowed the rider's face but intense red eyes cut through that shadow. 'Put away the gun. This is my property. I have every right to kill you.'

'It's your call,' Dehner's voice was toneless. 'If you holster your gun, I'll do the same with mine.'

Stacey Hooper's face became increasingly pale as Dehner and the newcomer faced each other with their guns in hand. For Stacey, time moved slower than a desert tortoise, but it was less than thirty seconds later that the man on horseback twirled his gun and holstered it.

Dehner returned his Colt to its holster without the fancy motions. 'Would you be Slushy Snow?'

'I am.' Slushy rode his horse to the rail, dismounted, and spoke again as he tethered it. 'Who are you?'

'The name is Rance Dehner, my friend is Stacey Hooper.'

'What do you want?' Snow pulled a roll of papers from one of his saddlebags.

'I'm a detective investigating the bank hold-up—'

Snow's voice was a hard lash. 'What's to investigate? Lon Westlake's in jail.'

'Penelope Castle thinks he's innocent,' Dehner fired back.

Snow gave his companions a contemptuous smirk. 'A girl as beautiful as Penelope can say anything she wants and men will listen.' The smirk relaxed, becoming a straight line. 'Both Penelope and her father are good people. Good people always assume everyone else is good. That gets them in trouble … serious trouble…. OK, come in. I'll give you a few minutes, nothing more.'

No emotion showed on Dehner's face but he was shocked. He had expected a man with the name of Slushy Snow to be white-haired and scraggly-bearded. The man who lived in the cabin was over six feet four with dark hair and a thin mustache that ran to both sides of his chin forming a horseshoe. His face had a wan look and his eyes appeared to be permanently bloodshot. Slushy Snow spent little time sleeping.

The man was lean and as he walked to the front door, his body swayed a bit like a whip in motion. 'Harland had this place fixed up for me before I arrived. Don't expect coffee, I'm not the hospitable type.'

Slushy pulled out a key. The thick, wooden door was a

recent addition and was secured by a large, heavy lock.

As they followed Slushy Snow into the cabin, Dehner and Stacey Hooper had to remain stationary while their reluctant host made his way to the room's one window, which occupied the left side wall. He removed a bar from the window and opened the shutters.

A blast of sunlight revealed that the cabin boasted two long tables; one of them was covered with maps. Four chairs were scattered about, two of them holding stacks of books. A large cot was propped against the right wall of the cabin. An oven, which stood in the far left corner, appeared unused. Slushy Snow didn't cook his own meals.

Stacey pointed at the books. 'I see you are a man who enjoys the comfort of a good book. I like to relax with Charles Dickens myself—'

'I don't read for pleasure, I read to make money and there is nothing comforting about it.' He tossed his roll of papers onto the empty table. 'I'm a mining engineer. Those books are written by engineers, not limey novelists. I've just come from the mines and I have a lot of work to do. So, say what you have to say and be gone.'

'You must work for Castle Mining,' Dehner said.

'Yes. Harland Castle hired me about four weeks ago. His people told him that the mine was about played out. He called me in to confirm that fact.'

'And what did you find?'

'They were right. The mine is less than three months away from being useless. But I found a rich vein in an old mine the company owns but has abandoned.'

A sneer creased the engineer's face. 'So, you see, Mr Dehner, in order to free Lon Westlake you will have to discredit the testimony of a man who has just saved this town from ruin. Were it not for me, people would already be pulling out.'

Slushy's harsh demeanor seemed to have no impact on Stacey Hooper, whose face beamed cordiality. 'You are a man totally dedicated to his calling, Mr Snow. The very high calling of being an engineer whose intellect provides a livelihood for an entire town.'

Slushy gave Hooper a hostile glare. The gambler didn't seem to notice. He continued in a cheerful voice. 'So, strictly as a matter of curiosity, of course, why were you standing across from the bank that night? I know the charming town of Hard Stone well. In order to have been across the street from the bank, you must have been perched in front of Linda's Shop for Ladies. The shop was closed, but I suppose you could have been window shopping to purchase a hat or other item for a very special lady in your life. Am I correct?'

Snow's hostility turned to hatred, which flared from his eyes. 'That's none of your business!'

'Yes, it is our business, Mr Snow,' Dehner replied. 'A man's freedom will be decided by your testimony.'

'And as I understand it, there will be a trial next week.' Stacey's manner remained relentlessly perky. 'Talking over this matter with us will give you some practice for the big show.'

Slushy Snow reached into his jacket pocket to pull out a tobacco pouch and papers. As he built his smoke Dehner wondered if the man was using the time to calm his temper or to concoct the details of his story. Of course, it could have been both.

The engineer waited until he had taken the first puff on his cigarette before he spoke. 'I have trouble sleeping. That particular night, I felt tired but restless. I was thinking about all that had to be done to reopen the mine. So I went into town, hoping some time in a saloon, a few drinks and a little poker, would be relaxing.'

'Of course, I understand,' Stacey Hooper bubbled. 'What with all of those important thoughts piled on your tired brain you mistook Linda's Shop for Ladies for the Lucky Miner Saloon or one of the town's other fine drinking establishments.'

Snow's upper lip became a thin line over his teeth. He took a step toward his visitors. 'The Lucky Miner was boring, nothing but a collection of fools. The other bars would be the same. So I left the saloon and took a walk. That's when I saw Lon Westlake come running out of the bank.' He took a few long strides to the door and opened it. 'Good day, gentlemen.'

Rance took on Stacey Hooper's friendly demeanor. 'Thank you for your time, Mr Snow.'

Stacey stepped outside first. Rance was still in the doorway when he turned to face the engineer. 'I have to ask about your name—'

Slushy snapped his response. 'Snow is my real last name. When I was young my so-called schoolmates called me Slushy. The name stuck.'

Dehner stepped onto the porch. 'I guess the nickname doesn't bother you.'

The engineer continued to bare his teeth. 'I learned long ago that most people are fools and what they say comes from minds filled with crazy dreams and dark superstitions. You are about to find out all about that, Mr Dehner.'

'What do you mean?'

A loud laugh exploded from Slushy Snow as he slammed the door.

CHAPTER NINE

'I believe that in our brief visit with Mr Slushy Snow we succeeded in making the gentleman most uncomfortable. I must confess that our achievement leaves a smile on my lips and a song in my heart.'

Rance and Stacey were riding back to Hard Stone through a valley surrounded by rocky hills after departing from Snow's cabin. Dehner grinned at his companion. 'I think I know the reason you are so pleased with Slushy's discomfort.'

'Limey novelists indeed!' Stacey shouted, confirming Rance's theory. 'Any man who denies himself the works of Charles Dickens is a contemptuous fool.'

'I won't argue with you on that point. I think *A Tale of Two Cities* is—'

A shot ended Rance's literary musings. The bullet hit a rock directly in front of Stacey. The gambler's black gave a loud, panicked whinny and lifted onto its hind legs, throwing Stacey onto the ground.

As the black galloped off, Dehner's horse began to bolt. The detective fought to control his bay as another shot fired out, this one sailing over his head.

Rance figured there would be another shot and the next one may not miss. He quickly assessed the situation. The shooter had positioned himself well. He was on a high hill to their left, behind a boulder. The hill stood directly on the side of the trail. On the right side, Rance and Stacey were between two rises. They were completely exposed, and running for cover would be dangerous.

Stacey was on his feet, firing at the shooter with his

Colt .45. They needed a rifle. Dehner made a quick decision. He pulled his Winchester from its boot and hastily dismounted, allowing his horse to run off.

Dehner aimed quickly and fired the Winchester. The shot ricocheted off the boulder. The shooter could be seen ducking down.

'Good shooting, my friend,' Stacey said.

'Not really. I didn't even get the shooter's nose out of joint,' Dehner said as he levered the rifle.

'I never have understood that expression,' Hooper replied.

'I'll explain later; hit the ground!'

Both men dropped to the ground and rolled to the flat land beside the trail. They lay behind a scattering of rocks, which just barely covered their heads. 'Let's hope our friend up there is a poor shot,' Stacey said. 'We don't blend in with the dirt very well. We make rather easy targets.'

As if making Hooper's point a shot landed inches away, spurting dirt in their direction. Dehner lifted his body slightly and fired the Winchester, then once again flattened himself on the ground.

Hooper's voice took on a critical edge. 'I'm afraid our opponent's nose remains perfectly in place. Perhaps we should—'

'Quiet!' Dehner snapped. 'I think I hear voices.'

Rance and Stacey fell silent and didn't move. The voices came from the top of the hill. Two men seemed to be having an argument. Dehner could only make out fragments of what was being said.

'... what in hell ...'

'... shut ... damn mouth ... Move ...'

Sounds of horses galloping off filled the valley; Rance

and Stacey exchanged confused stares. The gambler spoke first. 'It appears there has been a rather fortuitous development.'

'I hope you're right. This could be a trap. Let's stay where we are for a while then make our way very carefully up the hill. I'll go up the right side, you take the left.'

About fifteen minutes later, the two men began their trek. Dehner arrived at the top first and began to examine the area. A lizard rested on the boulder where the shooter had been. His head darted about quickly. He was very interested in something but not in the recent developments which had almost brought human slaughter to his territory.

The detective's eyes were on the ground when Stacey Hooper joined him. Rance shifted his gaze to the gambler. 'Spot anything unusual on your way up?'

Stacey took a handkerchief from the side pocket of his jacket and wiped his brow. 'No, just the usual snakes and spiders. Wretched things. The so-called beauties of nature are so overrated.'

Dehner continued to speak as much to himself as to his companion. 'There were two riders here. Their horses were tethered far apart.'

'Fascinating.'

'The way I have it figured, the shooter was working alone but while he was busy trying to kill us, someone surprised him and made him stop. After that, they rode off together.'

Stacey returned his handkerchief to its pocket. 'Judging from the harsh tone of the voices we heard, our Good Samaritan must have forced the shooter to forgo his evil deeds. But why?'

'Don't know,' Rance admitted. 'If the second rider had been a lawman, you'd think he would have checked to make sure we were all right. But whoever it was didn't want us to see him or the jasper who was trying to kill us.'

'The ground is too rocky for them to have left much of a trail.'

'Yes,' Dehner said. 'My guess is they are returning to Hard Stone.'

'Why?'

Dehner took off his hat and ran a hand across his forehead. 'The shooter wants to kill us. The Good Samaritan didn't seem all that offended by the notion. He just wanted to wait.'

'Wait for what?'

'I don't know.' Dehner put his hat back on. 'We'd better start walking. Remember that creek between here and the town? Our horses are probably there.'

'Yes, of course. If we start now we might make it back to Hard Stone in time for our appointment with Mr Lon Westlake.'

As the two men made their way down the hill, Dehner noticed that his companion appeared to be his usual self, a man mildly amused by life. 'Stacey, I still can't quite understand why you are so interested in helping out on this case.'

'You are right in not putting too much stock in my altruistic instincts. My motives are more philosophic.'

'Philosophic?'

'Indeed! I wish to prove that Mr Thomas Hobbs was only two-thirds right. Life is short and brutish, but it need not always be nasty. Life can be fun if you refuse to let it be dull. And, despite your puritan notions, Rance, life never seems to be dull when you are around.'

CHAPTER TEN

'I'm deeply disappointed by your unfamiliarity with the origin of the expression, *nose out of joint*, Stacey.' Dehner spoke with mock alarm as the two men rode into Hard Stone. 'After all, the expression comes from a British writer and soldier.'

'It must be someone outside of my immediate circle,' Hooper shot back.

'Perhaps. The gent's name was Barnaby Rich. He lived in the late fifteen hundreds. The expression is a visual way of describing someone who is highly displeased—'

'Yes, yes, I am impressed with your knowledge; now please refrain from parading it.'

Dehner did feel a little embarrassed. 'Sorry. I'm not an educated man like you, Stacey, just a man who has a lot of time to read.'

Hooper was still a tad irritated. 'Well, if you would take my advice and—'

Running footsteps pounded the boardwalk beside them. The coat of a black suit was flapping as its owner dodged between his fellow citizens, shouting an occasional 'Sorry,' when he collided with another pedestrian.

'Rather uncouth fellow,' Stacey commented.

'His name is Thorton Nevin. He's the pastor of Hard Stone's only church.'

'Leave it to you to have already struck up an acquaintance with the town's only clergyman.'

Dehner was now watching the parson with intense interest. 'Something's gone wrong.'

Rance and Stacey followed Reverend Nevin's clumsy run.

As they neared Westlake's General Store, a man's angry voice could be heard shouting from inside. Thorton Nevin scrambled through the store's door. The detective and the gambler tied up their horses at a hitch rail and ran inside, only a few steps behind the clergyman.

Tom was literally jumping up and down in front of the store's counter. Bottles rattled on the shelves as if the earth itself was trembling. 'It ain't right! Ya should let the dead lie in peace! All you care 'bout is money, Harland Castle. Well, I'm not gonna let ya open the mine!'

'Who is that?' Stacey whispered to the detective.

'I only know his first name … Tom. He does chores for the church, like grave-digging.'

Stacey continued to whisper. 'Let's hope some dear soul departs soon. It appears that Tom needs some exercise.'

Tom had stopped jumping but his face was red and both of his hands were folded into fists. The target of his wrath, Harland Castle, was standing erect in a stoic manner behind the counter. He was a man in the upper reaches of middle age who stood at about five and a half feet with a face covered by a salt-and-pepper beard. The salt appeared to be rapidly pushing out the pepper.

Penelope Castle stood beside her father with one hand placed on his arm. An older man and woman were at the far side of the store watching with great interest; trips to the general store were rarely this entertaining.

Reverend Nevin raised his index finger at Tom as he spoke in a voice of reprimand. 'You disobeyed me!'

Tom took a step backwards as if avoiding a punch. 'I'll get that door fixed. Plenty of time.'

'I told you not to come to the store today because the devil's got you in a hellish mood. You promised you wouldn't. You told me you were going to fix the door. You'd stay away because you knew Mr Castle would be here. So what happens? The moment I check up on you, I find that you are gone. I had to put aside my work and run here.'

Tom's face contorted. He looked like he might break out crying. 'Ya should help me! They're dancin' on the grave of your brother too!'

'TOM!'

The ferocity of Thorton Nevin's voice caused even Stacey Hooper's eyebrows to jump.

Tom's body folded at the middle. His voice wavered as he spoke to the floor. 'OK. I'll fix the door.'

'And what do you say to Mr Castle and his daughter?'

Tom remained silent.

Reverend Nevin put more force into his voice. 'What do you say to them?'

Tom kept his eyes on the floor. 'I'm sorry.'

'I accept your apology, Tom.' Harland Castle spoke softly. 'These are very hard days for all of us. But better times lie ahead. You'll see.'

Penelope Castle gave Tom a kind smile and Reverend Nevin a nod of thanks. Dehner got the impression that this was not the first time Thorton Nevin had rescued Tom from his own anger.

Reverend Nevin departed with Tom a step or two behind him. Dehner stepped outside the store and watched the two men make their way down the boardwalk to the church. The sight made him uncomfortable. Tom remained behind Reverend Nevin with his head bowed. The detective's face twitched. There seemed to be an invisible chain around Tom's neck, which Thorton Nevin was holding.

'Excuse us.' The older couple that had been inside the

store passed by Dehner, their arms wrapped around their purchases.

Rance stepped back into Westlake's General Store. Penelope had already introduced her father to Stacey Hooper and now presented Rance as, 'The detective who has agreed to help Lon.'

Harland Castle's body slumped as he shook hands with Dehner. The mine owner was obviously relaxing a little after his encounter with Tom. The men exchanged pleasantries then Dehner got to what was on his mind. 'How did Tom know you were here in the store, Mr Castle?'

Harland smiled whimsically and looked at this daughter, who answered the detective's question. 'I checked with Sheriff Kendall this morning to make sure it would be OK for us to meet with Lon. Emery Brown, his deputy, was there at the time. Both men do rounds and Tom frequently walks around town. One of them must have told him that we would be meeting here at about two in the afternoon and then going to the jail.'

Dehner nodded his head. 'What did Tom mean when he shouted about letting the dead lie in peace and dancing on graves?'

The smiles vanished from the faces of Harland Castle and his daughter. Harland answered this question. 'Tom and Reverend Nevin share a tragedy in their lives.'

Harland cleared his throat. 'Jess Nevin used to be a miner here in Hard Stone. In fact, he wrote his brother, Thorton, when the founder of our town's church died and we needed a new parson. Tom's brother, Virgil Flynn, was also a miner.'

'You speak of both men in the past tense,' Dehner said.

'Yes.' Castle inhaled deeply and then continued. 'About

45

six months ago, we closed one of our mines because it was played out, or so we thought. I still don't know what went wrong, but on the last day of work in the mine there was an explosion and the eastern section caved in. Four men perished, but we were only able to retrieve two bodies. That mine is the grave of two miners.'

'Virgil Flynn and Jess Nevin,' Dehner said.

Harland picked a small splinter off of the store's counter and tossed it to the floor. 'Now we are reopening that mine. Thorton understands. But Tom ... well ... you've seen what Tom is like.'

'Tom thinks you are desecrating his brother's grave,' Dehner said.

'Yes and, in a way, he may be right.' This time, Harland slapped the counter. 'The whole situation makes me uneasy. But the future of Hard Stone is at stake! There is a rich vein in that old mine that runs west. The eastern section will remain closed, but we have to reopen that mine or this whole town will be dead.'

Harland Castle's use of the word 'dead' seemed to startle him. The mine owner looked about nervously but said nothing.

'One more question,' Dehner persisted. 'The relationship between Thorton Nevin and Tom Flynn, did it begin after the mine caved in?'

Harland still looked unsettled. His daughter answered hastily. 'No. Reverend Thorton can be abrupt at times but he's really a fine man. I'm afraid Tom is what some people call the town fool. His brother, Virgil, just couldn't handle him. Reverend Thorton sort of took responsibility for Tom. Tom lives with the pastor. The church pays Tom a bit for doing chores. Oh, good....'

Ralph Morris, the store clerk, stepped hastily inside, apologizing for being late from his lunch. Penelope assured him all was well.

Ralph was left alone with the store as Penelope and the three men made their way to the jail.

CHAPTER ELEVEN

Both the sheriff and his deputy were in the office when Penelope Castle entered, followed by her retinue. The posture of Deputy Emery Brown immediately straightened as he turned from a gun rack behind the office's one desk and yanked off his hat.

'Afternoon, Miss Castle!'

'Good afternoon, Deputy Brown, Sheriff Kendall.' Penelope introduced Rance and Stacey to the two lawmen. As she did so, Dehner quickly assessed the two officers. Emery Brown was a wiry man of average height, thick sandy hair, and brown eyes that danced when they beheld Penelope Castle.

Pete Kendall's eyes looked permanently tired. The sheriff had stood up from his desk when Penelope entered, and had taken off his hat, movements that appeared entirely mechanical. The sheriff stood a tad shorter than his deputy. His face held a battered look that came from decades as a lawman. His body was muscular and his once dark hair was now streaked with gray.

'Pleased to meet you, gents.' The sheriff spoke to Rance and Stacey in a voice that communicated strong displeasure. He turned to Penelope Castle. 'I heard you'd employed a detective, Miss Castle.'

'Lon Westlake is an innocent man, Sheriff. I intend to do everything in my power to prove that fact.'

'You have ever' right to hire a detective, Miss Kendall!' Emery bellowed. 'You know, I'm thinking about maybe joining up with the Pinkertons someday.'

Pete Kendall cringed at his deputy's remark. He then looked at Stacey, which didn't improve his mood any. 'And what is your interest in this matter, Mr Hooper?'

'Why, that of a concerned citizen, Sheriff Kendall.'

Anger flared over Kendall's face. He gave Hooper a harsh glare and there was nothing mechanical about it.

Penelope took advantage of the sheriff's distraction and smiled pleasantly at Emery. 'Deputy, do you think it would be possible for us to meet with Lon inside his cell? Trying to hold a conversation across iron bars can be difficult.'

'Why sure, Miss Castle.' Emery pulled out a side drawer of the desk and grabbed a ring of keys. 'I'll take you there right now.'

Kendall's eyes left Hooper and dropped to his desktop. The sheriff obviously did not approve of his deputy's actions but didn't want to embarrass him in front of others, especially in front of a pretty girl. He remained silent, caressing his right leg, which seemed to be giving him some trouble, as Emery led a parade through the door that led to the jail cells.

There were four cells in the jail area. In one of them, a bald man lay on a cot, snoring loudly. He seemed to be sleeping off drink. Two of the cells were vacant.

'You got some company, Lon!' Emery smiled broadly as he unlocked the other occupied cell and allowed Penelope and her three escorts to enter. Lon Westlake got up from the cot and tossed the book he had been reading onto it. He and Penelope embraced each other while Rance, Stacey, and Harland Castle studied their hands.

Emery felt out of the picture and tried to get back into it. 'I believe you're innocent, Lon! Yessir, you're just not the type to rob banks. Makes no never mind to me what the evidence says ... I'll try to prove you innocent!'

Lon and Penelope continued to embrace. Penelope was crying. Emery continued, 'Well, I know you folks got stuff to talk about.' He slammed the door shut loudly and locked it. 'Just give me a shout when you're finished.' He walked not too quickly back to the office area.

Lon and Penelope unraveled themselves slowly. Penelope spoke to her fiancé as she fingered away tears. 'You've got one of Hard Stone's two lawmen trying to prove you innocent.'

Westlake gave a caustic laugh. 'No one in this town would rather see me sentenced to twenty years in a federal prison than Emery Brown. That way, he'd have you to himself.'

'No he wouldn't,' the young woman replied.

A more businesslike atmosphere settled over the group as Penelope introduced 'Detective Rance Dehner and his assistant Stacey Hooper.' Stacey's face betrayed irritation at being given a secondary role but he didn't make an issue of it.

Lon Westlake stood as a testament to the fact that the job of storekeeper was more physically demanding than many people realized. He was thin but his body was hard with roped muscles. He had a large forehead and blue eyes that radiated intelligence. His appearance was surprisingly neat; only his blond hair, which appeared unkempt, betrayed the days he had spent in jail.

'Lon, if we're going to help you we need to know everything you can tell us about that bank robbery,' Dehner said.

'I don't have that much to tell!' Westlake began to walk around the cell. Everyone else shuffled about, allowing him room, as the prisoner related his story. 'I was sleeping on the sofa in my living room, late at night, when there was a hard knock on the door. It was Emery Brown. I let him in, of course. He didn't say anything about believing I was innocent that night! He said that the bank had been held up an hour or so back and an eyewitness had identified me as the thief. I told him he was crazy!'

'Do you often sleep on the living room sofa?' Dehner asked.

'Yes. I read myself to sleep. Reading is easier on the sofa.'

'And you sleep in your regular clothes?'

Lon answered Dehner's question in a resigned voice. 'Yes. I clean up and change in the morning.'

Dehner continued, 'How many people know about your sleeping habits?'

Westlake stopped pacing and stared into space as if thinking the question over. 'About everyone, I suppose. I get kidded a lot for being a bookworm. I've probably mentioned that I read myself to sleep while on the sofa to a lot of the folks that came into the store.'

Dehner pulled on his ear for a moment then changed direction with his questions. 'So, Sheriff Kendall wasn't with Emery Brown when Brown came to arrest you?'

Westlake began to walk around again. 'That's what I thought at first! A few minutes after Brown arrived Pete Kendall came storming into the house. His gun was drawn. He had checked the horse I keep in a small corral behind the house. Kendall said the horse had been ridden hard within the last couple of hours. He accused me of robbing the bank, riding a short distance out of town and hiding the money, then riding back into town. He demanded to know where I had stashed the money.'

'When was the last time you remember riding your horse?' the detective asked.

'The bank was robbed on a Thursday night, Mr Dehner. I hadn't been on that horse since the previous Sunday afternoon when Penelope and I rode out for a picnic. And, before you ask, I didn't loan the horse out to anyone.'

'Did you check on the animal when you got home that Thursday night?'

'No. I was tired. I went right to the sofa and my book.'

Stacey Hooper spoke up in a playful voice. 'This entire incident shows Hard Stone's officers of the law in a bad light. Lon, you said that when Emery Brown arrived at your front door, he told you that the bank had been robbed about an hour before, correct?'

Lon Westlake nodded his head.

'Hard Stone is hardly a huge city,' Stacey continued. 'Why did it take the gendarmes so long to arrest you?'

Penelope began to answer Hooper's question. 'Immediately after the hold-up, George Conklin and Slushy Snow went to the sheriff's office to report the robbery. There was no one in the office. Mr Conklin knows that Sheriff Kendall likes to always have someone there....'

Lon threw up his hands and continued the narrative. 'Conklin figured there must have been trouble of some kind requiring both men—that sort of trouble usually takes place in one of the bars. So Conklin and Slushy headed for the Lucky Miner. No lawmen there. The next stop was the Silver Coin, same story. Finally, they headed toward the opposite end of town and the Red Dog Saloon. That's where they found the sheriff and his deputy.'

Harland Castle spoke for the first time since arriving at the sheriff's office. 'Sheriff Kendall figured Lon's house was the logical first place to look. I think he was surprised, at first, to find him there. But when he saw how hard Lon's Appaloosa had been ridden … well … he went by what his eyes saw—'

Stacey interrupted with a loud laugh. He held up an index finger as if addressing a class. 'Remember what Plato told us about the eye: "Its vision is confused and its beliefs shifting, and it seems to lack intelligence."'

Silence blanketed the group for a moment. Lon Westlake's face went pale as he spoke to his fiancée. 'These are the men who are going to help me?'

The door leading to the office area swung open and Emery Brown re-entered. 'Sorry, folks but time's up.' He keyed open the jail cell and motioned for the guests to leave. 'Not my idea; Sheriff Kendall's orders.'

'Perhaps it is just as well.' Harland Castle spoke as the three men shuffled out of the cell.

The deputy watched nervously as Lon and Penelope once again embraced. His eyes remained on Penelope as she reluctantly left the cell. 'I sure meant what I said before, Miss Castle. I'll do everything I can to prove Lon Westlake innocent.' He slammed the jail door shut without looking at the prisoner.

Outside the sheriff's office, Harland Castle excused himself after checking his pocket watch. 'I have an important meeting back at the house with Mr Snow. He should be arriving in about fifteen minutes.'

Penelope smiled and waved at Harland as he hurried off, then turned to her two companions. 'This is a very tense time for my father, which is why I need to speak with you, Mr Dehner ... and Mr Hooper.'

Stacey smiled politely at his last moment inclusion, 'What is it you need to talk with us about, Miss Castle?'

'The bank robbery has placed Castle Mining in a very precarious position,' the young woman explained. 'The company has little funding right now. Father struggles to meet payroll every week. Right now, Harland Castle is not collecting a salary. He has managed to talk Slushy Snow into working without pay until the old mine reopens.'

'Or until the money from the hold-up is recovered and the company once again becomes more solvent,' Stacey added.

Penelope continued, 'Yes, but meanwhile Father and I are living off our savings and ... you see ... Father was going to pay a prominent lawyer from Denver to come here and defend Lon.'

Dehner spoke softly, 'And that is no longer possible.'

Penelope pressed her lips together and nodded her head. 'Mr Dehner, could you defend Lon?'

The question stunned Rance. 'But doesn't Hard Stone have any lawyers?!'

'One,' Penelope shot back, 'and he serves as the town's prosecutor.'

'But—'

'Father has suggested we get Reverend Nevin. Thorton Nevin is an educated man and, I'm sure, a good person but some people in Hard Stone think he's a cracked pot. I don't want him defending Lon, I want you to do it, Mr Dehner. Please.'

Now, it was Dehner's turn to press his lips and nod his head. 'OK, I'll do everything I can to prove Lon innocent.'

Penelope's face beamed with a bright smile and damp eyes. 'Thank you! And Mr Hooper, I know you will be a tremendous help to Mr Dehner. I only ask of you one thing.'

Stacey's eyebrows lifted in curiosity. 'I will gladly fulfill any request you make.'

The young woman's smile became a straight line. 'P-l-e-a-s-e, no more quotes from Plato!'

CHAPTER TWELVE

'Stacey, it is time for us to have a chat with a banker,' Dehner spoke after Penelope had departed for her work at the general store.

Dehner and Hooper passed by the Silver Coin Saloon on their way to the bank and heard a conversation between two men coming out from between the batwings.

'We'll leave at sunup tomarra mornin', and this time we start searchin' 'round that patch of cottonwoods.'

'Let's look at those trees careful like. Maybe Westlake marked one of 'em and buried the loot there.'

Dehner smiled as he and Hooper continued down the boardwalk. 'A one thousand dollar reward certainly encourages civic-minded behavior.'

'Don't be so sure, my friend. I suspect many of Hard Stone's good citizens would grab that money and head for a good life somewhere across the border.'

As Dehner and Hooper entered the bank, they were greeted by a burly man only a few pounds away from being called fat. He was wearing two guns, both of which were tied low. A recent shave and new clothes only partially detracted from his thuggish appearance. He had been leaning on a side wall by the entrance. Excitement came into his eyes as he saw the newcomers. His day had been long and dull; now there would be some fun at last.

He stood in front of Dehner and Hooper, making it impossible for them to advance any further into the bank. 'You gents have an account here?'

Stacey smiled pleasantly. 'I fail to see how that is any of your business, ah....'

'My name is Frank Cole, people call me Cole.'

'Very well, Cole,' the gambler continued. 'I am Stacey Hooper, this is Rance Dehner. You can call us *Mister* Hooper and *Mister* Dehner. Now—'

'I'm the bank guard here and I'm tellin' both of you misters to get out!'

'We are here to ask Mr Conklin a few questions about the hold-up.' Dehner's eyes shifted to the bank manager. Conklin was sitting at his desk with eyes down, presumably reading an important document, totally unaware of the little drama going on in his bank. Rance was certain it was an act.

A smirk crossed Cole's face, 'You jaspers got an appointment?'

'No,' Dehner snapped.

'Well, Mr Conklin don't see nobody without an appointment. And he ain't makin' any new appointments till next week. So, you two jaspers can jus' haul your—'

Stacey Hooper had heard enough. He pushed past the guard and headed for George Conklin. Cole's right hand went for one of his guns but never got there. Dehner slammed a fist into the gunman's nose. A sound of crunching bones was followed by a bellow of pain and a loud thump as Cole collided with the floor. Blood spurted onto Cole's chin as Dehner jerked the guns from his holsters.

'Freeze, both of you!' George Conklin was now standing behind his desk. The Remington in his hand was old but still looked like it could do a lot of damage. 'I'm ordering you two men to leave … immediately. If you don't, I'll have you both arrested.'

Dehner was certain Conklin could make good on his threat. He and Stacey would do Lon Westlake no good if they occupied the cell next to his.

The detective walked slowly to Conklin's desk and dropped Cole's pistols onto it. 'You can return these to your guard, after he gets back from the doctor.' Dehner glanced at Hooper, who was now standing behind him. 'We'll leave, Mr Conklin. But we still have some questions and we're not going to rest until we get the answers.'

Rance looked quickly around the bank. One of the tellers was now crouched over Frank Cole, who was holding a handkerchief over his nose. Another teller remained behind his cage. There were three customers, who were watching the proceedings with wide eyes.

After they had left the bank, Stacey Hooper shook his head in anger. 'Banks are supposed to be the foundation of a civilization. George Conklin hiring a ruffian like Frank Cole is an act of sacrilege!'

The detective quickly looked back. Cole was now on his feet and like everyone else in the bank, was staring intently at Hooper and Dehner. 'Well, Stacey, in the West there is a certain rule of civilization you'd be smart to abide.'

'And what is that?'

'Always watch your back.'

CHAPTER THIRTEEN

Dehner and Stacey Hooper were enjoying a second cup of coffee in Fleming's Restaurant. The dinner hour was almost over and there were only a few other customers in the establishment. Still, Hooper kept his voice low as he spoke.

'Rance, have you considered the possibility that this Lon Westlake could be guilty as charged? I mean, he seems a decent fellow and all, but many a good man has been brought down by the temptation of filthy lucre.'

The detective also kept his voice low. 'The bank wasn't robbed.'

'What do you mean?'

'Ever heard of a man named Tully Brooks?'

Stacey chuckled at the name. 'Yes, of course. From what I read in the papers, Mr Brooks is an authority on bank robberies and similar pursuits.'

'I killed him two days ago.'

'Nothing personal, I'm sure.' Hooper sipped his coffee.

'Before he died, Brooks told me he had been part of a phony bank hold-up in Hard Stone. He rode out of town carrying saddlebags stuffed with newspapers while George Conklin fired shots in his direction and shouted that the bank was being robbed.'

'The deathbed confession of a repentant sinner.' Stacey's eyebrows lifted in appreciation. 'Well, well, that does explain Mr Conklin's reluctance to meet with us a few hours back.'

Hooper gulped down his remaining coffee, removed two cigars from his suit pocket, and handed one to Dehner, 'The perfect conclusion to a fine meal.'

Rance accepted the stogie and placed it in his shirt pocket. 'Thanks. I don't smoke much but I may need this later on. A good cigar improves concentration.'

'I will be concentrating too, my friend.' Stacey spoke as both men got up from the table. 'I'm having a friendly game of cards tonight at the Lucky Miner. Care to join the fun?'

'Playing cards with you is an education, Stacey, but not fun. I'll pass.'

Approaching the Lucky Miner, Stacey Hooper spotted Slushy Snow standing in front of the saloon. The face of the mining engineer hardened as Hooper stepped onto the boardwalk.

'Surprised to see you here tonight,' Snow's voice conveyed anger, not surprise. 'Thought you'd be in your room, playing at make-believe with some story book.'

'What I seek tonight is a little fun at the card table,' Stacey assumed a fake friendliness. 'It will be a gentleman's game, of course, but I'm willing to be charitable and allow you in, that is, if you feel up to the challenge.'

Snow took a step toward the gambler, giving Stacey a whiff of his breath. Slushy Snow was getting an early start on his drinking. 'I could beat you at … ' Snow suddenly stepped back. 'You're not worth the trouble.'

'You're good at tough talk, Mr Snow. Not so good at backing up your words.'

'I've got nothing to say to you. Go away.'

Stacey stepped into the Lucky Miner, feeling confused. His confrontation with Slushy Snow had been more than a bit odd. Snow had appeared relieved when the gambler left him alone. The mining engineer remained outside the saloon. He seemed to be waiting for someone, but whom?

Stacey exchanged words of friendly bravado with the men he had come to play cards with. He assured them he would be ready for 'a friendly game or two' following 'a brief after-dinner drink.'

He ordered a beer and leaned against the mahogany as the barkeep poured it for him. He glanced outside where he could spot Slushy Snow's shoulder.

Carrying his mug to a far side of the saloon, he pretended to take an interest in the action at a roulette wheel. From that vantage point he had a better view of what was going on immediately outside the batwings.

Matters quickly got interesting. An older, well-dressed man with a large handlebar mustache approached Slushy Snow. Handlebar was accompanied by two younger men with threatening smirks: guns for hire.

The well-dressed man smiled in a manner that conveyed threat rather than cordiality. There was a brief conversation, after which the four men walked away from the saloon.

Feigning indifference, Stacey strolled quickly toward the batwings. Looking over the doors he saw Snow and his companions walking in the direction of the hotel, but he couldn't be sure that was where they were actually headed.

'Tomorrow sometime I must report this to my dear detective friend,' he whispered to himself. 'But right now, I have to make a living.' He headed for the card table and his night's work.

After leaving Fleming's Restaurant, Dehner walked down the boardwalk to nowhere in particular. He was trying to sort out the details of the case.

'Maybe I need a little help with my concentration right now,' he whispered to himself as he stepped to the edge of the boardwalk, struck a match against his thumbnail, and fired up the cigar Stacey had given him.

As he inhaled on the stogie, his nerves tightened. The moment he had stopped walking he had heard footsteps behind him begin to slow and then stop completely. Not all footsteps; two miners now passed by the detective as they continued what appeared to be a trek to the Silver Coin Saloon. But the detective was certain there had been at least one other person behind him.

Cigar in hand, Dehner resumed his walk. Steps once again sounded softly behind him, or at least someone was trying to keep his steps soft. He smiled inwardly. It was pretty hard to follow someone on a boardwalk with loose boards and his apparent adversary was an amateur who didn't have the sense to use the dirt street.

Clouds rolled over a half moon, creating an image vaguely resembling a horse. Dehner paused, inhaled on his cigar, and pretended to take an interest in the heavens. But his thoughts were on earth. When he stopped, so did someone behind him: he was definitely being followed.

The detective continued his journey. He was now several steps behind the two miners who, as he had guessed, stepped into the Silver Coin. As they did, three barflies stumbled through the batwings and onto the boardwalk. Their voices were loud and angry.

'That fat fool won't give us no credit and we's payin' customers most times.'

'Let's git to the Red Dog; they know how to treat a man right!'

'How 'bout the Lucky Miner, they's good people....'

Dehner nodded politely to the three large men as he stepped around them. There was a break in the boardwalk.

Rance pivoted into the small alley between the Silver Coin and a hardware store. He tossed the cigar to the ground and toed it out. A bobbing red flame could expose his ploy.

The detective listened carefully as the three barflies continued their discussion on which saloon would most appreciate the business of three drunks who didn't have any money. He could hear boots shuffling around the deadbeats and recognized the figure that stepped in to the mouth of the alley.

Dehner grabbed Slade Pierson, pulled him into the alley, and slammed the aspiring gunslick against a side wall of the Silver Coin. The half moon provided enough light for the detective to observe that Pierson's face was still swollen from being whacked the previous night by Dehner's Colt.

'Why are you following me, Pierson?'

'What in hell ... you're loco!'

'I'm a busy man, Pierson. I haven't got time for nonsense. Why are you following me? If you don't talk fast, I'll break your arm.'

Panic widened Slade's eyes. 'I'm not sayin' nothin'.'

That remark told the detective plenty. Slade Pierson was a scared man. Scared of getting his arm broken and more scared of letting out the name of the big shot that was paying him. Dehner needed to up the ante.

'Slade, I think your days in this town are over. But before you ride off, you're telling me the name of the gent who hired you.'

'Nobody hire—'

Dehner continued, 'Because if you don't, Slade, I'll not only break your arm, I'll break every finger on both of your hands. That will end your chances of ever being a gun-fighter. You'll have to get a job somewhere. Think about it,

Slade, you'll have to work steady.'

'George Conklin!'

His face didn't show it, but Rance was pleased that Pierson gave in so easily. Slade Pierson was a saddlebum. Within a year or two, he'd probably die on a saloon floor after a gunfight with another man who wasn't quite as drunk as he was.

But still, Dehner didn't want to break his arm.

Dehner and Slade Pierson stood in the front yard of a well-built house. But the surrounding yard displayed total neglect; there were no flowers or shrubs planted anywhere.

'You're sure George Conklin lives alone?'

'Yep,' Pierson kept his eyes on the ground.

'And you say that about two hours ago he found you in a saloon and told you to come to his place in an hour?'

'Uh huh.'

'When you got here, he paid you to rough me up a bit and then bring me to his house?'

'Yep.'

'And when he gave you the cash, he was alone, from what you could tell?'

Slade nodded his head. 'Conklin spends some time with doves. But he always takes care of that in one of the cribs.'

The detective pushed Pierson up to the front of the house. Dehner pounded his fist several times on the door. Heavy footsteps sounded from inside and then the door was flung open.

'What in the devil's name is—'

Rance pushed Slade Pierson into the bank manager. The collision dropped both men to the floor.

Dehner palmed his Colt as Conklin began to reach

inside his coat pocket. 'Don't even think about it, Conklin, keep both of your hands in plain sight.'

The bank manager did what he was told. Rance shifted his gaze to Pierson. 'Leave. I'd better not see you in Hard Stone again.'

Slade Pierson scrambled to his feet and out the door. Dehner gave Conklin a slanted smile. 'I should have told him to give you your money back. He was supposed to scare me. All he did was get me mad at the man who hired him.'

Conklin was on his feet, brushing off his suit. 'I don't know what you're talking about.'

'Yes you do.' Dehner holstered his gun. 'This afternoon, you had that thug you call a bank guard block me from talking to you.'

'He was just trying to do his job—'

'When did you hire an armed guard for a small town bank?'

George Conklin's face twitched in embarrassment. 'I'm only a manager. The bank is owned by a large outfit in Denver. After the robbery, they ordered me to hire a guard.'

'And you gave the new hire my name and description and told him to boot me the moment I stepped into the bank. When that didn't work out so well, you paid Slade Pierson to deliver me to your home complete with fresh bruises. Why?'

Conklin worked his hands together as if they were in pain. His posture suddenly improved and he tried to speak in a businesslike voice. 'Let's talk in my library.'

As they made their way down a short hallway, Dehner kept his right hand loose and close to his Colt. The detective suspected that George Conklin's library had few books but probably a gun or two stashed in desk drawers. But he figured Conklin's real motive for retiring to the library was to regain some control. The bank manager wanted to take charge of the situation.

As he entered the room, Dehner saw that his first speculation was correct; the library didn't even have bookshelves. The uncarpeted room contained a large desk with a chair both behind and in front of it and little else. But the desk looked like it received a lot of use. Papers and letters, some opened, some not, were strewn over it.

Conklin strutted behind his desk and smiled broadly. 'I understand you're working for Penelope Castle, is that correct, Mr Dehner?'

'Yes.'

'What's she paying you?'

'That's none of your business.'

The bank manager gave a loud, artificial laugh. 'Sounds like Penelope is rewarding you with more than just money.'

'Look, Conklin, if I want to waste time listening to bad jokes, I'll go to a saloon. At least the barflies have the excuse of being drunk.'

George's smile became less broad. 'OK then, I'll get down to business. I'll pay you seven hundred and fifty dollars to ride out of town first thing tomorrow morning.'

'How will you pay me?'

'In cash. Tonight. Right now. It's easy money. Whaddya say?'

'I say no. There are just so many interesting things going on to keep me in Hard Stone for a while.'

'Like what?'

'Being a detective is an odd calling. Two days ago I killed a man who was sort of a friend. His name was Tully Brooks. Every heard of him?'

Conklin shook his head a little too vigorously. 'No.'

'You're lying. You paid Tully Brooks to pretend he was robbing the Westward Bank of Hard Stone.'

'Brooks told you that?'

'Yes, shortly before he died from a bullet I put in him.'

'And you believed him?!'

Dehner replied in a firm monotone. 'Yes.'

Conklin's businesslike demeanor slid from his body, to be replaced by tension and desperation. His eyes moved to the top desk drawer. 'There are some papers I want—'

'Keep your hands where I can see them, Conklin!'

A fierceness came into the banker's face. 'What Tully Brooks said is worthless. He was a killer and a thief. You'll never prove a thing.'

Dehner gave the banker a mocking smile. 'You're half right, George. Tully's claims are worthless in a legal sense. But I know he was telling the truth and it will only take me a few days to get the evidence. Oh, and since you're so interested in my clients, I now have another one.'

'Who's that?'

'That large outfit in Denver you were talking about, the one that owns the bank you manage.'

Panic surged in Conklin's eyes. 'The Westward Bank of Commerce!'

'Yep. They smell a rat in your story about the hold-up. They've hired the Lowrie Detective Agency to look into it. I received a telegram from my boss after leaving the bank this afternoon. We'll be talking again soon.'

Dehner turned and began to saunter out of the library. He suddenly stopped and drew his Colt .45 as he did a fast swing back to where he was facing the banker. 'Toss the gun on the floor, Conklin!'

Conklin didn't quite have the pistol out of his shoulder

holster. He slowly removed it and followed Rance's orders. 'You're going to be sorry you didn't take the money, Dehner. Very sorry. There's a lot going on in this town you know nothing about.'

'I don't like to be threatened, Conklin. And I don't much like it when people hire thugs to push me around. You try something like that again and I'll kill you.'

Dehner watched the banker carefully as he stepped out of the library. Conklin's eyes were filled with an intense hatred but his hands were shaking.

CHAPTER FOURTEEN

Tom Flynn looked out of the window of Thorton Nevin's small house toward the church which stood beside it. He saw the shadowy figures of six women leaving through the front door. He couldn't distinguish their faces in the darkness but two of them had sharp, high-pitched voices which cut through the night air.

'Looks like the old hags are finally done,' Tom said.

Reverend Nevin looked up from the table where he had been working on a sermon. 'Tom, the women in the Ladies Missionary Alliance are good people. They have done some very nice things for you.'

'They cackle like a bunch of old hens, especially that Etta Fleming.'

The irritation in Thorton's voice gained more force. 'Tom, you've been acting badly since lunch, now stop it.'

'Etta ain't suppose ta make me do dishes. It ain't right.'

'Etta and Andy Fleming give you a free lunch at their

restaurant every day. One of their usual people was sick today and they had you help clean dishes. Nothing wrong with that.'

'I always gotta eat in the kitchen. Can't eat out in front with the people.'

The clergyman had heard enough. 'I don't blame them for making you eat in the kitchen. The way you act, always complaining, you'd drive the paying customers away. Now, get over to the church and do your chores!'

Tom stomped loudly out of the house, slamming the door behind him. Thorton Nevin sighed deeply and massaged his forehead with both hands. Taking care of Tom Flynn was the right thing to do, he was sure of that. But doing the right thing was draining him. Tom seemed to be taking over his life. He had no time for....

The pastor smiled whimsically. Maybe he should practice what he preached and not complain so much even if most of the complaining was done inside his mind. He whispered a joke told to him, years ago, by a fellow student of the Bible, 'Lord give me patience, and give it to me now!'

The joke and the memories of his days as a student made him feel better, but only for a very few minutes.

As he reached the church, Tom saw that the front door had been left open. 'Crazy old biddies, ain't polite enough to close the door. Let Tom do it!'

He closed the door behind him. Two small windows, composed of ordinary glass, dotted each side wall of the church. Stained glass windows were a luxury in Colorado, limited primarily to Denver. A kerosene lamp was fastened beside each window. Tom's final duty of the night would be to put the lamps out.

The church contained fourteen pews; each could hold four people or, as Reverend Nevin put it, five very skinny people. A narrow aisle ran down the middle of the church dividing the pews into two rows of seven.

Tom clomped noisily down that aisle. His steps reverberated in the wooden building, which contained no carpet. A platform at the front held a piano and a pulpit. Tom stepped around that platform and through a door on the right side of it. He was in a short corridor that led to the pastor's office, or what was originally intended as the pastor's office. The church couldn't yet come up with the money for a desk so Thorton Nevin did most of his work at the plank table in his home.

Tom stepped into the office, colored yellow by the kerosene flame in one large light fixed to the back wall beside the room's one window. Near the light stood a circle of six chairs, which Tom had arranged earlier for the meeting of the Ladies Missionary Alliance. He put the chairs back against the wall, stacking three of them. The chairs were old and not alike. In all there were eleven battered chairs in the room, which could be brought out when the pews were filled. On Christmas Eve and Easter Sunday, the church borrowed more chairs from the Lucky Miner Saloon.

After attending to the chairs, Tom checked the floor. This week, none of the women had dropped a pencil or left her notes behind. He closed the window, then took a broom and heavy cloth from where they rested in a corner.

Back in the sanctuary of the church, Tom propped the broom against one of the pews, took the cloth and examined the side windows. They all looked a bit smoky. Maybe he should open them and let some air in while he swept.

He stopped suddenly as he approached one of the

windows: there seemed to be someone standing immediately outside the church. Tom rubbed the glass with a cloth. Yes, there was someone there and he was walking toward the window.

As the figure stepped closer, Tom started to yell in fear but it came out as an infantile squeak. He dropped the cloth. His mouth went dry. The rest of his body trembled.

The face of the figure now filled the window. Tom wanted to touch that face, not injure it, just touch it, to make sure it was real and not a ghost. The window exploded into shards of glass as he hurled his right hand through it.

The face in the window remained calm but its expression changed. The face smiled sympathetically at Tom as he withdrew his bleeding hand.

Tom Flynn began to shout hysterically as he ran from the church.

Reverend Nevin reread the passage in 2 Corinthians to make sure he was quoting the Apostle Paul correctly. He could hear Tom shouting about something and those shouts were getting nearer and nearer.

'What now?' the pastor said aloud. The Apostle Paul had written about a thorn in his flesh, though he never specified what the thorn was. Reverend Nevin had no doubt as to the source of his own personal thorn.

Tom ran into the house, splattering drops of blood. 'You gotta come! You gotta come!'

Thorton shot up from the table. 'Tom, what happened to your hand?'

'Never mind, Reverend, I saw him but it must have been a ghost—'

'Saw who?'

'Virgil! My brother, Virgil Flynn!'

Pain and anger coursed through Thorton Nevin. Couldn't Tom at least leave those painful memories alone? Nevin couldn't keep the anger from his voice. 'That's impossible! Virgil died in the same mining accident that claimed my brother, Jess. They're both buried in that mine. Now, stop babbling a lot of nonsense!'

Tom stomped one foot on the floor. 'I ain't lying! I ain't lying! You gotta come!'

Reverend Nevin took hold of his nerves. He realized Tom's fear was genuine. A calm approach was needed here. 'Of course, I'll come with you. I want you to tell me exactly what happened. I'm sure we will find out you've made a mistake.'

The half moon and the still lighted kerosenes in the church made a lantern unnecessary. As the two men left the house, Tom explained about seeing his brother's face in a church window while getting ready to sweep the sanctuary.

'You gotta believe me! I saw him!'

'I know you're not lying, Tom. You think you saw Virgil. But it was your imagination. Now, let's walk around the church a few times....'

Thorton Nevin guided Tom as they walked behind the church. A thick forest of trees bookended Hard Stone on the east and west sides. But the night was hot and still and the tree branches didn't stir.

As they came to the other side of the small building, Reverend Thorton pointed ahead. 'Is that the window where you think you saw this ... ghost?'

'Yes ... and I saw it. I wasn't thinking up nothing.'

'Let's take a closer look.'

As the clergyman took a step toward the window, Tom

inhaled sharply and grabbed his arm. 'Reverend, look!'

A figure had stepped out of the forest and now stood only a few yards away from the men. Moonlight seemed to cut the figure in half; one side was easily visible while the other remained in darkness.

'My God ...' Nevin's voice was raspy as if escaping through frozen cords. 'Oh, my dear God ...'

'That should do it, Tom.' Reverend Nevin spoke as he tied a second clean rag to Tom Flynn's hand. 'Be careful how you use that hand for a few days and it will heal soon.'

Tom and the pastor were sitting at the plank table. Both men were scared and both were trying to hide it. Tears puddled at the far corners of Tom's eyes. 'We shoulda gone into the woods with the sheriff. Help him find my brother's ghost.'

'That wasn't a ghost, Tom.'

'You thought so! You ran. You're yellow!'

'I'm not!' Once again, Thorton Nevin struggled to control his emotions. The clergyman admitted to himself that he was ashamed of his behavior. When he had spotted the strange figure that had stepped out from the woods he had, indeed, turned and made a run for the sheriff's office. Tom ran right behind him.

Nevin spoke in a low voice made wavy by his erratic breathing. 'Sheriff Kendall instructed us to return to the house while he ... investigated. Besides, you were losing quite a bit of blood; we needed to bandage that hand.'

'I know why my brother has come back as a ghost.'

'Tom, it wasn't—'

'He can't rest in peace because the mine is being opened up. Men are gonna be dancing on his grave. All because

71

some greedy jaspers—'

Sheriff Pete Kendall walked into the house without knocking. The cuffs of his old Levis were covered with burs accumulated in the woods.

Reverend Nevin stood up from the table. 'What did you find, Sheriff?'

'Nothing.'

'I see.' The clergyman looked down in embarrassment.

The lawman also looked uneasy. 'You know, gents, we don't get many warm nights here in Hard Stone. So, when we do get a couple weeks of hot weather...well...it can do some crazy things to a man's thinking.'

The Reverend looked unconvinced. 'But Virgil has ... had ... such a unique appearance. He was totally bald because of a childhood disease.'

'And there's that red line running down his forehead!' Tom shouted from where he was still sitting at the table. 'He got that in school when two bullies were making fun of me and pushing me around. Virgil fought those two bullies. One of them had a knife and slashed him on the forehead with it. Virgil took care of him good. But that cut never healed proper. And I saw it tonight. Don't nobody call me a liar.'

Thorton Nevin pressed his lips together before speaking. 'But, well, maybe our eyes did play tricks on us. Maybe we saw someone, maybe it was a drifter, a man who was hungry and coming to the church for some money to buy food.'

''Fraid not, Preacher,' the lawman replied. 'I looked over the ground around the church real careful. From the window where Tom said he saw the face and into the woods. There were no footprints, not a trace of anyone bein' out there.'

Tom sprang up from the table, waving his injured hand. The kerosene lights seemed to highlight the red blotch that oozed from the white rags. 'A ghost don't leave no footprints. I saw the ghost of my brother. He's come back to tell us something and we'd damn well better listen!'

CHAPTER FIFTEEN

George Conklin smiled to himself as he rode toward the mine. The conversations he had overheard at Fleming's Restaurant that morning still had him amused. The ghost of Virgil Flynn had appeared to Tom Flynn last night. Of course, it was no surprise that a halfwit believed in such superstitious blarney but, apparently, the sky pilot made the same claim. The bank manager figured he lived in a town of fools, but he wouldn't have to put up with the morons much longer.

Conklin slowed his black as he drew near the Castle Mining Operation. He dismounted and tied his horse to a dead tree. He removed a telescope from one of his saddlebags and strode quickly toward a large knoll, which he climbed stealthily. At the crest, he lay flat and used the telescope on the mining operation below. Yes, he was there: Slushy Snow. And, from what he could see, the mining engineer was behaving as usual: arrogantly barking out orders.

The bank manager closed the telescope and ran back to his horse. Slushy Snow had an unpredictable schedule. George knew he had to move quickly.

A ride of less than fifteen minutes was needed to get to Slushy Snow's cabin. The bank manager tied up his horse at the hitch rail and chuckled as he pulled a key from his pocket. He recalled the conversation with Harland Castle a month or so back.

Harland had been nervous, but then he often was nervous. 'George, I need your help. Slushy is OK with the cabin we have fixed up for him but he needs a lock.'

'What do you want me to do, give him directions to the hardware store?'

'Slushy wants a very strong lock. There's no time to order it. Now George, I know you have some extra locks at the bank....'

The bank manager went along with Harland's request. He didn't mention that he had two keys for the lock he had loaned to Mr Snow. He now placed one of those keys in the lock and entered the cabin.

The place stood dark. The cabin's one window was closed with a heavy metal bar running through the handles of the shutters.

'Slushy Snow is a man who wants and needs privacy,' George Conklin whispered to himself.

Conklin yanked a match from his pocket and struck it against the door. The small flame provided enough light for him to see the table covered with maps and drawings. He moved quickly to the table and began to examine everything there.

'Looking for something?'

The words streamed violently through George Conklin. His eyes skidded about the cabin.

'I'm over here.'

The bank manager looked in the direction of the voice. What he saw caused him to raise his left palm outward as if defending himself from a blow.

The strange figure gave a hard, mocking laugh. 'Your hand is shaking.'

George took a step backwards. 'It can't be ... you are ... you're Virgil....'

'Yes. And I bet you thought ghosts only appeared at night.'

The bank manager stumbled. As he hit the floor, a terrible pain scorched his wrist. The match had dropped into the sleeve of his coat. He managed to smother the flame in the coat cloth and crush the match stick, which was now a hot ash.

But George Conklin faced a peril much more dangerous than the burn on his arm. The dark outline of a figure now stood over him. His body trembled as he saw the shadow pull an object from his belt. Seconds later, Conklin realized the object was a knife.

Penelope Castle finished singing the last verse of a hymn as her hands gracefully moved from the piano keys. She received enthusiastic applause from the one other person in the room.

'Thank you, Father,' the young woman shook her head, displeased with herself. 'But I haven't been sleeping very well lately and my throat seems to have tightened up. I'll probably sound like a clucking chicken tomorrow morning.' She closed the cover on the piano.

Penelope and Harland Castle were observing a Saturday night custom. Using the piano in their living room, Penelope would sing the solo she would perform in church the next morning. Penelope was the church's piano player and only soloist.

Harland arose from a small sofa. 'You'll do just fine—'

He suddenly stopped speaking.

'What is it?' Penelope stood up from the piano and approached her father.

Harland was looking toward the large window in the room. 'I thought I saw someone come out of the woods and start walking toward the house.'

Penelope's head quickly turned in the direction of the window. 'Yes,' she said. 'Someone is coming. I ... I wonder....'

Penelope didn't dare speak her thoughts. Reverend Nevin and Tom claimed that on the previous night they had seen the ghost of Virgil Flynn. According to the two men, the ghost had vanished into the woods. Could this be...?

As the figure reached the window, Penelope cupped a hand over her mouth to stifle a cry.

'Virgil Flynn!' Harland spoke in a hoarse whisper.

The figure now glared at them from the other side of the window. His smile was mocking, with more than a hint of a threat. He slowly moved away, vanishing into the darkness.

Harland ran to the window and quickly looked out. He bolted for the Winchester, which lay across the front wall over a mantle. He broke the rifle to make sure that it was loaded, then closed it with a loud snap.

'Father, what are you going to do?' Penelope stepped toward her father.

'I don't believe in ghosts. Someone is playing us for fools. I intend to find out who.'

'Please, Father, let's get the sheriff.'

'You get Kendall. I'm going after that spook. Time is of the essence.' Harland moved toward the front door, stopping at a small table to light a lantern, which he held in his left hand as he cradled the Winchester in his right.

'I'm going with you, Father!'

'Get Sheriff Kendall!'

'I'm going with you!'

'No time to argue. Stay close by me.'

The two Castles scrambled outside, onto and then off the front porch. They scooted to the side of the house where Virgil Flynn had appeared, stopping briefly by the large window. A rustling sound came from the woods.

Father and daughter exchanged glances. 'Our ghost may have tripped over a log,' Harland said.

They quickly moved toward the woods. As they did, Penelope thought how lush and beautiful the trees appeared. The unusually warm weather had worked its magic. Greenery was not often found in a cold mining town like Hard Stone. Strange the things that run through your mind while you're chasing a ghost, Penelope thought.

Harland and his daughter slowed their pace as they entered the woods. They pushed against a tangle of branches. Vines ran across an old and rarely used path.

Sounds of a panicked retreat sounded nearby. Penelope looked hastily around her. 'I think I saw coyotes, two of them, running away. I guess we scared them off.'

'Let's keep moving, but be careful.' Like his daughter, Harland spoke in a whisper.

They pushed aside several more branches and then stopped. A small clearing stood before them with a huge tree in the middle. A corpse dangled from a rope that was attached to one of the tree's branches. The body was more than five yards off the ground. The feet and ankles were torn and bloody. The coyotes had made successful jumps at indulging in a snack.

Penelope looked to the sky and screamed. Harland put

an arm around her as his entire body seemed to go limp. 'Dear God … it's George Conklin.'

CHAPTER SIXTEEN

'Breakfast is ready,' Penelope declared with forced cheerfulness. Harland Castle came to the dining room table and sat down. He bowed his head while his daughter said grace. Upon opening his eyes, he commented on how good the food looked but he didn't put any of it on his plate. He was only interested in the coffee.

Sunup was almost a half hour away but both Castles had given up on getting any sleep. Penelope had hoped food might calm her father's nerves. 'Try to eat something.' The young woman's voice took on a slightly playful tone. 'After all, you don't want to fall asleep in church this morning.'

Father and daughter exchanged mechanical smiles as people do when they know things are bad and not about to get any better. Harland stirred his java as he spoke. 'Guess I need to pay attention in church, careful attention.'

'What do you mean?'

'I'm a bit confused about spiritual things. I mean, up until last night I was convinced ghosts didn't exist. Now, I'm not so sure.'

Penelope had been trying to eat some bacon in order to set a good example for her father. She gave up on the task and placed her fork on the plate. 'You think what we saw last night was not a real man; you think it was a ghost?'

Harland's eyes left his coffee cup and shifted to his daughter. 'Last night, did you take a close look at the ground outside the window or the area that leads to the woods?'

Penelope shook her head.

Harland's voice became intense, his eyes flamed. 'There was nothing there, no footprints, nothing! I talked with Kendall after he looked around. The only prints he found were ours!'

'Father, do you think a ghost killed George Conklin!?'

Harland Castle's eyes shifted downwards. He covered his face with his hands. 'I don't know ... I don't know ...'

Horst Weber limped slowly around the Castle mining operation. This was his last round of the shift and his favorite. Early daybreak provided just enough light to make a lantern unnecessary. He needed to carry only his old Sharps.

Weber had been injured in the explosion that claimed several lives and left two men buried in one of the mines. Weeks after the explosion, when it became obvious he could never work as a miner again, Harland Castle had offered him a job guarding the place at night.

Many of the townsfolk had scoffed at the notion and called it charity. One lady had even said to him, 'The railroads give their old men a gold watch. You get to stay up all night for the rest of your life.'

Weber stopped at the tracks that ran into the mine, which was still operational. He carefully inspected the ore cars. Last night was Saturday night, when men get some pretty crazy ideas about playing jokes.

Nothing wrong. Horst had carried out the inspection despite the fact that the mine would be closed on this day: Sunday.

As he moved on, he began to reflect on the irony of

how people regarded his job. After Tom and the preacher claimed to have seen the ghost of Virgil Flynn on Friday night, the same folks who had made fun of his job now urged Harland Castle to fire him and to find a young, healthy man to look after the mines at night.

He had gone to Mr Castle and volunteered to step aside. 'Sir, I know how important it bein' that the old mine gets opened back up and all. So, if ya'd rather have a young buck lookin' after things, I won't be complainin', not one little bit.'

Harland Castle had put a hand on his shoulder. 'I have complete confidence in you, Horst, but be extra careful. Somebody in this town seems to be trying to pull some dangerous mischief.'

Weber thought the ghost talk was a lot of silliness but, in a way, he hoped it was true. He had always liked Virgil Flynn. Oh, some folks say he was a terror when he got mad. But Virgil had been his friend. They had often enjoyed a few beers together after work.

Footsteps sounded from a distance, accompanied by an airy sing-song voice, as if someone couldn't decide whether to sing joyously or cry in despair. The sounds echoed off the large stones and seemed to come from the old mine, the one that would soon be reopened. There was no reason for anyone to be there at this time on a Sunday morning.

'No good reason,' Horst whispered.

The guard moved as fast as he could down a rocky slope to the second mine. But he had to proceed in a cautious manner; too quick a pace might cause him to fall. Reaching his destination, he leaned against a large boulder, one which towered over his head, and rubbed his left leg, which now throbbed with a sharp pain.

The footsteps had stopped but the eerie voice remained. Weber peeked around the boulder and spotted the preacher, Reverend Thorton Nevin. The guard's face crunched up as a myriad of thoughts played through his mind: What in tarnation did...?

Horst began to lose his balance; he had to drop his rifle and cling to the boulder in order to stay afoot. A good one half of his body slid past the large rock and could be seen by Nevin. Weber silently cursed himself as he limped back behind the stone. The preacher was saying something but in that strange voice he had been using earlier. He seemed to be totally caught up in his own world, not hearing the pebbles roll, or seeing the guard fighting to keep his balance.

Weber eyed his rifle, which lay safely on the ground. Let it stay there for the time being; he needed both hands on the boulder to find out just what was going on. Cautiously, he once again peered around the large stone.

Thorton Nevin's eyes were fixed on the mouth of the mine as if he expected someone to step out from the black abyss. There was an intense look on his face, which spooked Horst, but the guard no longer feared being spotted. The preacher didn't move his head in any direction. He was only interested in the darkness that fronted him.

Nevin's voice suddenly rose in a shout. 'Lord, you brought the ghost of Virgil Flynn to the land of the living as you did in the days of the Old Testament with the ghost of Samuel. Now, bring the ghost of my brother to me. I need to speak with Jess. Please....'

The preacher dropped to his knees, crying in anguish. Horst watched, experiencing fascination, revulsion, and sympathy.

The crying stopped. The preacher leaned back and stretched out his arms. 'Yes, I hear you, Jess. I will tell them. They won't want to hear it. People never want to hear the truth. But I will make them listen. I will make them listen this very day.'

He slowly rose to his feet. His footsteps were uncertain and he appeared to stagger a bit as he began to walk downwards toward town. The high-pitched mystical quality returned to his voice and once again bounced off the rocks. He spoke as if repeating a mantra. 'I will tell them. They don't want to hear but I will tell them.'

Weber stayed behind the rock until the clergyman was out of sight. His first thought was to report this whole matter to Harland Castle, but he brushed that notion off. Harland and Penelope Castle were pretty busy on Sunday mornings. They usually visited Lon Westlake before church and Penelope played the piano and sang in the service.

Besides, there was nothing here that couldn't wait. Maybe he'd say something to Harland after the service or when he saw him on Monday morning.

The guard picked up his gun and wiped away the loose dirt with his hand. He thought a man should attend church on Sunday morning. It just seemed the right thing to do. But he frequently didn't make it. The night work left him too tired and he didn't want to doze during the sermon.

But Horst Weber figured he wouldn't miss this morning's service. 'Got a feelin' I won't have no trouble stayin' awake on this Sunday.'

CHAPTER SEVENTEEN

Rance Dehner watched as the prisoner paced his cell. Lon Westlake looked very distraught. Dehner could understand why. The circuit judge would be arriving in Hard Stone tomorrow morning; the trial was set for the afternoon and now Lon's fiancée was babbling about spooks.

'Penelope, you know … you know I love you and I'd trust you on anything but this talk about the ghost of Virgil Flynn….'

Penelope briefly looked away from her fiancé as if embarrassed. When she faced him again, her eyes had a pleading quality. 'It all sounds so crazy but, Lon, I saw Virgil Flynn last night and so did Father.'

Four people were crowded into Lon Westlake's jail cell. They were the same four who had been there the last time Dehner saw the prisoner: Penelope and her father, the detective, and Stacey Hooper. Rance noted that the only conditions that made this visit different were the morning hour and the fact that there were now five drunks sleeping it off in the other cells.

Westlake stopped pacing. His mouth became a tight line in a pale face. He didn't want to argue with his fiancée over the matter of ghosts. 'Mr Dehner, you say you've examined George Conklin's body?'

'Yes, it's in that old shack behind the barber shop where they keep the dead bodies before burial.'

Lon ran a hand through his hair. 'And you say Conklin didn't die from hanging?'

'No. There are two puncture marks on the corpse.

George Conklin was stabbed to death by someone who knows how to use a knife. Conklin's clothes were streaked with blood.'

Westlake began to pace again. 'But why would anyone murder Conklin and then hang his corpse in the woods behind the Castle home?'

Harland's voice resounded in a loud manner. 'Remember, Lon, we may not be dealing with living men. Men who think like you and me. Virgil Flynn may have returned from the dead and we have no way of knowing what drives him.'

'What in the world is wrong with you, Harland? Do—' Westlake suddenly stood still and inhaled. He then spoke slowly. 'I'm sorry but I just can't buy all this ghost stuff.'

Dehner spoke in a calm manner. 'There is one obvious fact we may be overlooking.'

'Aha!' Stacey Hooper lifted an index finger. 'I have often said that my friend is the West's greatest detective. He is about to prove it. Rance will point to something that has been under our noses since the beginning of this unfortunate affair but which none of us has truly observed. My good friend will then employ this overlooked fact and use it to solve the case, just like C. Auguste Dupin did in Poe's *The Purloined Letter.*'

Silence greeted Stacey's observation. Penelope Castle grimaced. Rance noted, with some amusement, that Penelope seemed to grimace every time Stacey opened his mouth.

'I'm afraid Stacey has overestimated my skills,' Dehner said. 'But as I understand it, Virgil Flynn was completely bald as a result of a childhood disease.'

'Yes,' Penelope replied; her father and Lon nodded their heads.

Dehner continued: 'And there was a red mark running

down the middle of his forehead where he had been cut in a knife fight.'

The response was the same.

Dehner tossed both hands up. 'You don't have to be C. Auguste Dupin to know it would be easy for someone to pose as Virgil Flynn's ghost. People's attention would naturally go first to the hairless head and the red line on his forehead.'

'That's what I used to think!' Harland Castle's voice was a nervous shout. 'But Virgil left no footprints! I saw it for myself last night and the sheriff says the same thing happened when Virgil Flynn appeared at the church. How do you explain that, Mr Detective?!'

Dehner smiled sheepishly. 'I'm afraid I can't, Mr Castle, not yet.'

Stacey Hooper's voice remained cheerful. 'Perhaps we all need to read more Edgar Allan Poe.'

Harland's voice was not cheerful. 'I think we all need to be going. Church is starting soon.'

Rance shouted for Emery Brown to come unlock the jail cell while Penelope embraced Lon and promised him she would be back that afternoon. As they made their way out of the sheriff's office, Harland apologized to Dehner. 'I didn't mean to sound harsh.'

'I understand the pressure you are under, Mr Castle. What with your payroll being robbed, the problems with reopening the old mine, having your future son-in-law in jail, and finding a corpse hanging behind your house … well, you're entitled to be a bit grumpy now and again.'

Harland Castle smiled good-naturedly. His daughter took his arm and they headed north toward the church. Rance and Stacey began to follow behind them but Hooper motioned for his companion to move slowly.

'I'm going to church, Stacey. You can join me for lunch later if you'd like.'

'No need. I'll accompany you to the service.'

'Fine.' Rance quickened his pace.

Stacey again motioned for his friend to slow down. 'Rance, I have noticed the attention to detail involved in your work. For instance, there's the way you studied poor George's corpse in that wretched shack. It must have been most unpleasant. And there's the time you spent fussing about Mr Westlake's horse. You try to study every detail that comes your way and build a good defense for Lon Westlake. That has taken a lot of your time and is most admirable.'

'What is your point, Stacey?'

'This is Sunday morning, the time for 'Ye shall know the truth and the truth shall set you free'... that sort of thing.'

'Yes.'

'Well, good friend, your doubts about my staying in Hard Stone for altruistic reasons involving freedom for Lon Westlake are justified. For that matter, I haven't remained only for amusement as an earlier statement implied. There are certain other matters which may or may not pertain to this case.'

'I'm listening.' Dehner was happy to know that his friend was about to tell the full unvarnished truth. He was also nervous. If Stacey was opening up and being totally honest, he must be in a dangerous situation.

The atmosphere inside the church was nervous, fearful and filled with mourning. Many of the worshippers had just heard about George Conklin's murder.

Reverend Thorton Nevin added to the tension. His eyes

were inflamed and seemed to be looking at something no one else could see. While Penelope sang her solo, he couldn't remain seated but began to pace about the small platform.

Dehner and Stacey Hooper were sitting in a back pew. The gambler whispered to his friend, 'That clergyman is acting like Lon Westlake, like a man locked up in a cell.'

'Maybe, in a way, he is,' Dehner whispered back.

When Penelope was finished, Nevin didn't thank her as he normally did. He faced the congregation and began to speak to them angrily as if they all shared in the same hidden sin.

'I used to be like the rest of you. I worshipped in the temple of mammon. I put money first. I thought it fine to desecrate the graves of two fine men in order for a company to make a dirty profit. Oh yes, by all means, let's do whatever it takes to keep this town alive. Let the filthy lucre keep flowing.'

Thorton Nevin shook a fist at his audience. 'What good does it do if we gain the world and lose our souls?! We must stand up and demand Castle Mining Operations leave the old mine closed, to do otherwise is an act of blasphemy!'

A large brawny man, whose Sunday clothes looked too tight on him, stood up from a third-row pew. 'You're talkin' crazy, Preacher. Most miners, we got us families to care for. Don'tcha care nothin' for them? Maybe you only care 'bout the dead. Livin' folks who need food and clothin' don't interest you none.'

Tom Flynn shot up from where he had been sitting on the front pew and pointed a finger at the man who had interrupted the sermon. 'Shut up, Bill Hanson! Shut up! Ya got no right to speak in church.'

'I gotta right to speak up when some fool attacks the way I make a livin'!'

'Don't ya call the preacher a fool!' Tom Flynn began to walk in a threatening manner toward Hanson.

From the platform, Thorton Nevin thrust out his right arm as if trying to throw a blanket of calm over the situation. 'Tom, return to your pew, right now. Bill, sit down please, we all need to—'

Tom began to walk faster. 'Ya don't care nothing about my dead brother. All ya care about is putting money in your pocket.'

From where he was sitting in the back of the small church, Dehner couldn't see who threw the first punch although he did hear Bill Hanson's suit coat rip as he delivered a haymaker in Tom's direction. Chaos erupted as some people tried to separate the combatants; some people fled the premises and others watched the fun.

Dehner tried to make his way down a crowded aisle toward the two fighters. As he did, he noticed several men angrily yelling at each other. The detective was grateful that men didn't wear guns to church. Raw emotions were now ruling. One shot could set off a hailstorm of bullets.

A woman screamed as Bill Hanson frantically pushed people aside and ran out of the building. Tom Flynn was directly behind Hanson and knocking over anyone still foolish enough to be standing in the middle of the aisle. Dehner allowed Flynn to pass and then ran behind him.

Outside the church, Bill Hanson stumbled and fell. Hanson immediately saw Flynn coming toward him and realized the man was going to deliver a kick to his ribs. Hanson went into a fast roll but Tom's foot still scraped hard against his side.

Dehner stepped between Tom Flynn and his fallen opponent. 'Tom, settle down. You don't want to hurt—'

Dehner saw Tom's first punch and was able to duck it. The second swing, however, collided with his head and sent him staggering backwards. Through blurred vision he saw a crowd forming a circle around the fight. He heard a cacophony of dissonant shouts as the goliath that was Tom Flynn charged toward him.

Dehner swung his leg and landed a hard kick against Tom's knee. Instinctively the big man bent over, grabbing his knee and struggling to stay afoot. Dehner slammed two quick rabbit punches to Flynn's head. Goliath went down.

'Stop it, stop the fight!' The voice belonged to Sheriff Pete Kendall.

If Tom heard the lawman, he gave no indication of it. He gave Dehner a hateful glare as he scrambled to his feet, obviously getting ready for another charge.

A shot fired followed by screams. The crowd froze; even Tom stood still. Everyone had assumed no one in the group was armed.

All eyes went to Stacey Hooper. The gambler was holding a derringer, which he had just discharged into the air. 'Now that I have your attention, I direct you to my immediate right where Sheriff Pete Kendall has a few thoughts to share with you.'

Despite the circumstances, Dehner smiled at his friend's action and words. Stacey Hooper never went anywhere without a gun, including church.

Sheriff Kendall didn't smile. He was obviously irritated at having to depend on the gambler to get the attention of the crowd, but decided to make the best of it. 'I want all of you to go home and cool off. All of us are under a lot of strain, I know that, but turning on one another ain't the answer. Tom Flynn and Bill Hanson, both of you don't get in spitting distance of each other. If you do, I'll throw you in jail. I'm talking at you like you were schoolboys because that's the way you've been acting.'

The crowd retreated into silence. Men toed the ground with their boots and the women studied their hands. They seemed to be pausing a moment before following the sheriff's instructions to leave.

The sheriff spoke to Rance in a voice that was almost a whisper. 'Thanks for keeping those two fools apart, I'm a bit slow this morning.' He nodded downward. 'Gotta bad knee, and it bites me sometimes when I try to move quick.'

'Things like that seem to happen to a lawman,' Dehner replied sympathetically.

If Stacey Hooper sensed the sullenness around him, he gave no indication of it. He cheerfully addressed Thorton Nevin. 'Reverend, since the congregation is now assembled out here in front of the church, would you care to dismiss us with a benediction?'

Except for Rance Dehner, no one caught the humorous intent of Stacey's remark. The crowd looked at Thorton Nevin in a curious manner as if they had forgotten about the pastor and were now surprised to see him.

Nevin's mouth began to move but no words came out. He gazed downward and then turned his back on the people and ran into the church as if seeking shelter from a violent rain.

The crowd dispersed, not talking, and each going his own way.

CHAPTER EIGHTEEN

Five men stood awkwardly in the living room of Harland Castle's home: Rance Dehner, Stacey Hooper, Slushy Snow, Pete Kendall, and Will Bain, the town's newspaper man. Harland Castle was sitting in a large, comfortable chair. Harland had apologized several times to those assembled for not standing up: 'I'm feeling a bit weak right now.' His daughter was trying to be a gracious hostess, directing guests to a table with coffee, tea, and a plate of cookies.

Looking about to see that all who were invited were now present, Harland cleared his throat and started to speak. 'Thank you for coming, gentlemen. I'm sorry to inconvenience you but I have an announcement concerning a decision I have just made. You see after ... well ... we all know what happened at the church this morning and, of course, about the murder of George Conklin. I've done some very serious thinking and— Mr Bain, is it too late to give you an item for the newspaper, I know it comes out on Monday.'

'No sir.'

'Fine. I didn't want you gentlemen to be surprised by my announcement.' Harland paused for a moment and then picked up a piece of paper, which lay on his lap, and began to read. 'I have reluctantly come to the decision that I am not the man to guide Castle Mining Operations through this vital time of transition. I will immediately initiate a search to find a new owner for the company. I am confident that this process will be quick. I also have great confidence in the future of Hard Stone and regret that poor health doesn't allow me to be a more active participant in that future.'

Harland handed the paper to Will Bain. The other four

visitors looked at Penelope, as if wanting more information. Penelope obliged. 'What Father didn't say is he plans to leave Hard Stone completely after the company is sold.'

'Why, sir?' Will Bain asked.

'Well, once the company is in new hands there will be nothing for me to do in this town. And, I must confess, the harsh winters here are getting more difficult on these old bones.'

Will Bain wasn't convinced. 'But Mr Castle, you have lived in Hard Stone for many years, why—'

Penelope answered the reporter's question before he was finished asking it. 'My father has been very upset by the recent events in Hard Stone. He believes that he cannot be comfortable here anymore.'

Harland Castle nodded his head. 'Yes, my daughter is right. Much as I love this town, I need to leave it before my memories are overwhelmed by a bank robbery, a ghost, and the sight of George Conklin's body hanging from a noose. These last few weeks have taken a lot from me. I no longer have the energy or the desire to head up a large mining operation. It's time to give the reigns to younger hands.'

The reporter turned his attention to Penelope, 'And what about your future, Miss Castle?'

'I know Lon Westlake is innocent of any crime and I know a jury will agree with me. After Lon is set free, we will be married. Father wishes for us to move with him, probably to California, and start over there. I'll talk it over with Lon, of course, but we will probably move with Father.'

Dehner felt sorry for the young woman, whose voice trembled. Penelope Castle had a fiancé in jail and a father who seemed to be bordering on a breakdown.

'I need to get back to the *Sentinel* office,' Bain declared.

'Got a story to write and a newspaper to get out.'

None of the other guests were impressed by Will Bain's self-important manner but they seemed grateful for the opportunity to end an awkward meeting. Polite goodbyes were exchanged as the five men left the house.

As they walked down the porch steps of the Castle home, Dehner and Stacey Hooper heard a voice from behind them that was not polite. 'I need to talk with you gents, alone.'

The voice came from Slushy Snow. His eyes were still bloodshot and his demeanor was jittery. Rance recalled Stacey's description of Snow when he met the three strangers outside the Lucky Miner.

Dehner glanced at the other men, who were stepping through the gate of the small fence that surrounded the house. 'Sure, Mr Snow, I don't think our hosts will mind if we spend a few moments under the tree in their front yard.'

Slushy Snow lit a cigar as he stepped under the cotton-wood. Stacey Hooper noticed Snow's discomfort and smiled brightly at him, no doubt wanting to make the man feel worse. Dehner tried to study Slushy Snow more carefully to find out what had left his nerves so frazzled.

The mining engineer inhaled on his stogie before speaking to Dehner. 'Have your case ready for the trial tomorrow?'

'I hope so, but as you know, I'm not a lawyer. Hard Stone only has one lawyer and he serves as the prosecutor. What happens tomorrow will be in the tradition of a miner's court.'

Snow gave Stacey a hard stare. 'I suppose you are assist-ing Mr Dehner?'

Stacey's smile didn't diminish in the slightest. 'Indeed. And I have found that my reading of Charles Dickens has helped in this matter. Dickens once wrote, 'If there were no bad people there would be no good lawyers.' Rance and I are convinced there are some very bad people involved in this affair, but Lon Westlake is not one of them. By the way, that quote came from *The Old Curiosity Shop*. You really should read it.'

An intense anger flared in Slushy Snow's eyes but only briefly. Whatever dilemma he was in, it did not allow him the luxury of choosing his associates. 'Since you two are so interested in being good lawyers, be at my place tonight right after sundown.'

'Why?' Dehner asked.

'Do you want to help Lon Westlake or not? Just do what I say, both of you!'

Dehner's right arm made a quick sweep. 'There's no one around here. Anything you have to say, you can say it now.'

Slushy Snow once again inhaled and puffed a large stream of smoke. He seemed to be speaking to the cloud he had created as it quickly dissipated. 'There are a lot of bad people here, very bad ... people you only think you know. Both of you, do what I say.'

He walked away quickly and didn't turn back.

CHAPTER NINETEEN

The sky still provided some gray light as Rance and Stacey rode toward Slushy Snow's cabin, enough light for Stacey to note the expression on his companion's face. 'You appear to be in deep thought, my friend.'

'Well, to begin with, Lon's trial starts tomorrow.' Dehner

sighed and continued, 'And then there is the matter of locating the money which *wasn't* stolen from the bank, to keep my boss at the Lowrie Detective Agency happy. And, of course, there is the murder of the bank manager. Yep, I've got a few things on my mind.'

'Perhaps you have given far too much thought to our meeting with Mr Snow.' Stacey's voice took on a pious tone. 'I suspect this is just a shameful attempt by a man who is little more than a ruffian to make some easy money. He lied about seeing Westlake rob the bank. Now, he will claim to have some new insight, which could set the prisoner free, an insight that he will share. For a price, of course.'

'I don't think so.'

'And why not?'

'For one, in order to have such an insight, Snow would have to admit he had been lying previously. I can't see him doing that.'

'Point well taken.'

'And then there is the matter of you, Stacey.'

'What do you mean?'

'You are not one of Slushy Snow's favorite people. In fact, the man hates you.'

Hooper laughed with delight. 'I know.'

'And yet, when he talked with us this afternoon, Snow emphasized that he wanted both of us at this meeting. Even though you goaded him with your Charles Dickens talk, he was very insistent we both show up at his place tonight.'

'Another point well taken; you have given me some sketchy details but no firm facts to back up your theory regarding our get together tonight with Mr Slushy Snow.'

'You could say I'm building a theory. I think it might be connected with the ... ah ... confession you made to me this morning before church.'

A touch of confusion dropped onto Stacey's amused expression. 'Perhaps the unfortunate episode from my past does relate to our meeting tonight.'

Dehner also looked a tad confused. 'Like I said, I'm building a theory—'

'You have little time left for your construction. We have arrived at Mr Snow's domicile.'

The two men dismounted and tied up their horses at the hitch rail in front of Snow's large cabin. Dehner noted that Snow's horse, a pinto, was also tethered at the rack.

'Slushy has a corral in the back of his cabin, but he has a horse in front, saddled and ready to ride,' Dehner whispered to the gambler.

'Mr Snow has never impressed me as a man who observes protocol and good manners. He is rude to people, he is probably rude to horses.'

Black had almost completely supplanted the gray in the sky as Rance and Stacey stepped onto the porch of the cabin. The moon was becoming more prominent and a scattering of stars was now easily visible.

Dehner tapped lightly on the door and was immediately greeted with a 'Come in.' Slushy had obviously heard them ride up.

As he opened the door, Dehner heard the large lock bang against it. The lock hung closed on the inside handle of the door.

The detective's eyes did a quick survey of his surroundings. The cabin's one window on the left wall was opened to alleviate the heat. Dehner smiled inwardly. He had hoped that would be the case. Slushy Snow sat on one of the cabin's two tables, near the right side of the cabin. A lantern perched beside him, providing a patch of flickering light.

'You're right on time, gents, please close the door.'

Dehner complied. He and Stacey Hooper walked toward Snow.

'We are here as you requested, Mr Snow,' the detective said. 'You claimed you had something to tell us that might be of interest.'

Slushy Snow gave a loud, mocking laugh as he stood up from the table. 'Oh yes, I've got something I think will hold your interest.'

'Botha you jaspers turn around, hands up.' The voice was high-pitched with childlike excitement. Dehner and Hooper did what they were told. They were looking at a figure that stood as an outline against the darkness of the cabin. The shadow was a little more than average height and giggling.

Slushy Snow added to the merriment by chortling as he spoke. 'Dehner, you and the limey are even more stupid than I thought. You walked right into a trap like two mules walking toward an empty trough.'

The mining engineer took a few steps toward the back wall. Bullets were about to fly from his unnamed accomplice and he didn't want to take a stray one.

Dehner ignored Snow and spoke to the shadow. 'Friend, you've got yourself mixed up in some very serious trouble. Where's your horse?'

The figure seemed to twitch in the darkness. 'Ain't nona your business.'

'Where's your horse?' Dehner repeated.

The shadow quickly used his gun hand as a pointer, 'Outback, in the corral.' The gun barrel again pointed at Dehner and Hooper.

'Leave now.' Dehner nodded his head toward the front

door. 'Ride far away from here and don't come back. You won't get another chance.'

The giggling became a guffaw. 'The way I figger it, I got me all the chances I want. You fellers are the ones running outta chances. Yep, dead men don't git chances to do nothing.'

The shadow took a deep breath and raised his gun hand. A voice boomed from the open window. 'Drop the gun now!'

'What?' The dark figure's voice was a screech. Like a child whose favorite toy had just been taken away from him.

The voice from the window became even louder. 'This is the law. I'm deputy Emery Brown. Slushy Snow, step away from the wall to where I can see you better. Keep your hands high.'

'Sure,' Snow began to walk in the direction of Dehner and Hooper. 'You got things a little confused, Deputy.'

'I believe all of the confusion stems from you, Mr Snow.' Stacey's voice bounced with delight. 'Rance and I set up a bit of a trap ourselves.'

A loud scream exploded across the cabin. The other men cringed as the shadow pivoted and two fast flames crossed between the dark figure and the window. The shadow screamed again, this time in pain.

Emery Brown jumped inside the cabin through the window. 'Drop the gun. I don't want to kill you.'

The gunman staggered, his voice sounding more than ever like that of a child. 'I got me somebody I gotta kill—'

Rance, Stacey, and Slushy Snow all dropped to the floor. A red-orange streak flew across the cabin, cutting into the far right corner of the ceiling. As he hit the wood, Dehner drew his Colt and purposely fired over the gunman's head.

Like Emery Brown, he didn't want to kill the man. He thought the gunman, if kept alive, could be a witness for the defense at the trial of Lon Westlake.

Dehner had, a few hours before, communicated this notion to Stacey Hooper and the deputy. Emery Brown now stood only a few feet away from the figure who continued to weave about in the darkness.

'Drop the gun, mister!' Brown ordered. 'I ain't saying it again.'

'Pa … Pa … sorry, Pa. Wanted to do right fer ya … sorry.…' The figure began to wilt, firing a shot into the floor and then collapsing.

Rance and Stacey buoyed themselves to their feet and scrambled toward Emery Brown, who was crouched over the fallen gunman. Dehner still had his Colt in hand and made several quick glances backward.

'Is he alive?' Dehner shouted the question as he gently touched Brown's shoulder.

A quick succession of bangs sounded in the cabin as Slushy Snow ran outside.

'Damn!' This time Dehner's shout was angry but his face filled with contentment as hoofbeats could be heard from the hitch rail.

The detective signaled for Stacey Hooper to join him as he ran outside and fired two bullets harmlessly in the general direction of the galloping pinto. 'Hell, he got away.' Dehner hoped the rider could hear him. 'It's too dark, there's no sense trying to catch him!'

Stacey Hooper gave his companion a lopsided grin. 'I would rate your performance as mediocre, at best. However, your audience of one, Mr Slushy Snow, is unsophisticated. I suspect he has never been inside a decent theater. Your severely limited acting skills were probably adequate for the occasion. But I fail to see the purpose behind this aspect of the charade.'

Dehner holstered his gun. 'A scheme Slushy Snow was part of is beginning to fall apart and he knows it. I have a pretty good idea where he's headed. I'm following him, but first I need to check on the health of a man who tried to kill us.'

When Rance and Stacey reentered the cabin, they saw that Emery Brown had located a second lantern. A beam of light now stood on each side of the body that lay on the floor. A wispy cloud was forming above that light and an acrid smell now permeated the cabin.

Brown anticipated Dehner's question. 'This man is alive, but barely. He only got shot once but the bullet is deep and close to the heart. We can't move him and there isn't time to get a doctor. We'll have to do what we can here. I've yanked out some bullets before.'

'So have I,' Stacey added.

'I had hoped Emery could have arrested him when he went for his horse,' Dehner said. 'That didn't work. You two will have to do the doctoring. I'm riding out for where I'm sure Slushy Snow is headed.'

The gambler looked doubtful. 'And exactly what is motivating Mr Snow to go to this particular location?'

'Fear and greed.'

The doubt vanished from Stacey's face. 'Ah, fear and greed, both quite dependable when assessing human nature. You are obviously on the right track, my friend, hurry off!'

CHAPTER TWENTY

As Dehner approached the mine, he could hear a horse nickering. The detective silently cursed himself and hoped Slushy's horse hadn't just sounded a warning.

He dismounted and tethered his bay with a heavy stone. There was a scraggly bush nearby with enough leaves for the horse to chew on. He then proceeded on foot up a broad dirt trail to the mine that had been closed. The mining engineer had left his pinto in front of the mine, not concerned about anyone spotting it.

'Maybe my acting isn't so bad, after all,' Dehner whispered to himself. Slushy Snow had thought no one was on his trail but did Snow hear his horse nickering and now have some second thoughts in that regard?

The detective slowly approached the large dark cavity, listening for any sounds that might come from the interior. How far inside that cave had Snow gone?

'Put yer hands up mister, now!' A voice yelled behind him, and Dehner's hopes of surprising Slushy Snow began to fade fast.

'Turn 'round real slow, like.'

Dehner followed orders and found himself facing an elderly man with a withered right leg. A Sharps was cradled in his right arm. He held a lantern high in his left hand. 'I recognize you, sir, but I don't think we've been introduced, the name is Rance Dehner.'

The old man was several yards away from Dehner and began to limp toward him. 'I'm Horst Weber, I guard these here mines at night.'

Dehner moved quickly toward the guard. No sense in

101

adding to the man's problems and the further away from the mine they were the better.

Both men stopped when they were just a few feet from each other. Horst looked over the newcomer carefully. 'Rance Dehner, I recognize ya, ya handled that situation at the church this morning real good.'

'Thanks, Horst. Say, think you could point your rifle in a different direction?'

Dehner had spoken to the guard in a low, soft voice. Horst replied in kind, 'Sure.' He pointed the gun to his side and placed the lantern on the ground. 'I've been hearin' some prime talk 'bout ya from Penelope Castle; she says you're a detective, that right?'

'Yep.'

'Pinkerton?'

'No. I'm with the Lowrie Detective Agency. We give the Pinkertons some competition.'

The guard looked pleased. 'The Pinkertons they do them some union bustin' and that jest ain't right.'

Horst Weber was a man who welcomed conversation. Dehner decided a little talk could be helpful. 'I don't care for union busting myself, and I like following wayward husbands and wives even less. That's why I work for the Lowrie Agency.'

As he spoke, Dehner repositioned himself so he could look directly at the mine. Horst Weber did the same. 'Are you familiar with a guy named Slushy Snow?' the detective asked.

Weber turned his head and sent a brown streak of saliva to the ground with a force that seemed to at least partially answer the question. 'Yep, ya'd think with a name like that a man would be friendly like. Hell, Slushy Snow is a mean one.'

'Does he go inside the mine at night very often?'

'He comes now and agin'. I spot that pinto of his some-times.' Horst pointed at the mine. 'When the pinto is there a lantern that hangs outside the mine entrance is gone and I know Slushy Snow is inside.'

'Do you ever go inside to see what he's doing?'

Horst kept his voice low but a new intensity came into it. 'And lose my job? No sir! Mr Castle tole me Slushy Snow can come and go as he pleases. I'm jest to stay outta his way.'

'Do many of the miners work in this mine during the day?'

'None of them do! Slushy Snow makes sure of that. No one gets to enter the mine 'till he says it's ready. The fellers work in the other mine and that's it.'

Dehner stared at the mine entrance and wondered how much of this conversation Snow was hearing. He reckoned at this point it didn't make much difference. Vague notions were bouncing about in his head trying to become solid and form a pattern.

'So, no one ever goes into this mine except Slushy Snow?'

'Well ... there was one time ... it was kinda special, like.'

'What do you mean?'

'It was 'bout a month back. I was doin' my first round when I saw a passel of horses in front of the old mine. Sheriff Pete Kendall hisself was standin' in front of the place like he was guardin' the nags or someth'n'. I started walkin' toward him ta find out what's up but I never got the chance to open my mouth.'

'Why not?'

'Well, 'bout the time I get within talkin' distance, Slushy Snow steps outta the mine laughin' like a drunken miner on Saturday night. Never forget that sight. Hell, it's the only time I saw that jasper smile, never mind laugh.'

'Was he by himself?'

'No sir! Mr Harland Castle and George Conklin was also there, along with two swells. At first, I thought the swells was from the East, they was dressed so high hat but I found out different.'

'How?'

Horst smiled at the memory. 'The two swells was happy as pigs in mud. Laughin' it up with Mr Castle, the banker, and Slushy Snow. The swells didn't walk none too steady, though. While Sheriff Kendall was helpin' 'em onto their horses, Mr Castle walks over to me and puts a hand on my shoulder. He whispers, "Horst, these are investors from San Francisco. They're puttin' big money into the company. Sometimes, alcohol is the oil that keeps a business movin'." After that, he winks at me then gets back with the others.'

'Was Mr Castle drunk when he said that?'

'Na. He'd had a few drinks but he wasn't in shoutin' distance of bein' drunk. I suspect the same was true of George Conklin and Slushy Snow.'

The notions in Dehner's head were beginning to come into better focus. 'What do you know about the inside of the mine?'

'Plenty, usta work in there. Walk in 'bout ten yards and the mine forms sorta of a T. The left side is where an explosion took place; it's closed off after a few feet. But the right side is jest dandy, runs from here to China. That's where they found them the new vein.'

'Thanks. Slushy Snow was involved in an attempted murder not much more than an hour ago. I'm going in after him.'

The guard tensed up. 'Reckon I should go with ya.'

Rance felt a lot of respect and a touch of sympathy for a man who wanted desperately to prove himself useful in a tight spot. But Dehner didn't really know Horst Weber well and couldn't risk putting him in a dangerous situation.

'I think I can handle Slushy Snow, but this situation calls for law. I need to explain to a lawman why he needs to jail Snow and jail him tonight. Could you ride into town and get the sheriff?'

A film of disappointment passed over Weber's eyes, but he quickly nodded his head accepting the responsibility given to him. 'Sure. I'll get myself inta town and back here with Pete Kendall soon as I can.'

'Thanks Horst, take Slushy's pinto.'

The opportunity to ride such a fine horse did seem to lift the guard's spirits. He put out the lantern that sat on the ground and then laid his Sharps against a nearby rock. 'Could ya sorta keep an eye on that 'till I get back?'

'Sure.'

Dehner pretended to check his Colt to make sure it was fully loaded while Weber slowly and awkwardly mounted the horse. The guard waved as he rode off.

'Even with his injury, Horst Weber is a fine horseman,' Dehner said to himself. 'He'll be back with the sheriff soon.' Dehner didn't regard that as good news but felt he had done the only thing he could.

The detective stepped carefully toward the mine entrance. Slushy Snow probably had some access to water. He could hold out for a few days in there—maybe more than a few. Of course he could eventually be starved out. But Lon Westlake's trial started tomorrow and Dehner needed to get the truth out of a lying eye witness.

Rance Dehner entered the mine.

CHAPTER TWENTY-ONE

Colt .45 in hand, Dehner slowly moved deeper into the mine, allowing his eyes to adjust to the darkness. He couldn't carry Horst's lantern with him or even strike a match. Both would make him an easy target.

The dirt under his feet was hard and becoming increasingly rocky. The slightest sound sent out waves of echoes. The detective paused and listened carefully. He could hear an erratic dripping of water coming from the direction of his right side and not too far away. He was probably getting close to the top bar of that T Horst Weber had told him about.

The detective continued his cautious steps. No light shone anywhere. That was hardly a surprise; Slushy Snow would have extinguished his lantern.

Dehner wondered about the Slushy Snow he was now stalking. Was this the cold, hard and precise mining engineer he and Stacey had originally dealt with or was this the shaky, uncertain man they had encountered earlier in the day?

A loud, sharp bang reverberated on Dehner's left side and seemed to answer the question. His adversary was attempting the oldest trick in the book, throwing a rock to give a false impression of where he was hiding. Dehner picked up a stone and hurled it to his left, hoping Snow would think he had fallen for it and was advancing toward the left side of the T.

It worked. Two red lances flashed across the cave creating waves of deafening sounds. Dehner took advantage of the roars and unleashed a painful yell. With the reverberations from gunshots exploding all around, Slushy Snow couldn't possibly determine the direction of Dehner's bellow.

The noise in the cave gradually faded and died. Rance didn't move. Several minutes of silence were followed by a low swishing sound. Dehner thought a match had been struck. A modest hint of light appeared several feet in front of him and gradually grew stronger. A hand carrying a lantern broke from out of the darkness like a grotesque firefly.

The hand remained suspended in mid-air. Slushy Snow was looking for Dehner's corpse. Rance couldn't be certain but he thought most of Snow's body was safely around the right turn in the mine. In a moment, Snow would realize he had been tricked and step backwards. The detective's first shot had to count.

Dehner took careful aim and hurled a bullet into Snow's left hand. The engineer screamed. Dropping the lantern, he retreated backwards and was now out of sight.

The detective could hear low cries. Slushy Snow was in pain and losing blood. Now might be a good time to rush him.

But the lantern Snow had dropped still splayed light in front of the entrance to the right side of the mine. An intruder would make an easy target.

A weak voice called out, 'Dehner.'

'Yes.'

'I'm hurt bad. Real bad. I think I might lose a hand.'

'If it's sympathy you're after, you are talking to the wrong man.'

'Look, Dehner, I want to surrender. I can help you defend Westlake, prove him innocent. I know plenty about what's been going on. All I ask is that you help me stop the bleeding and get me to a doc.'

'Throw out your gun and you've got a deal.'

A gun landed in a shard of kerosene yellow. Dehner walked cautiously into the light where he could see into the right branch of the mine. Slushy Snow was sitting on the ground. The engineer had taken off his brown coat and loosened his string tie. An ashen face held eyes intense with hatred or desperation, maybe both. He looked at Rance and held up the bloody mess that was his left hand. 'You can put away your Colt .45, Mr Detective, I'm finished.

Dehner holstered his weapon. 'Don't do anything foolish, Snow. I'm warning you.'

'If I lose much more blood, I won't be able to do much of anything, foolish or otherwise.' He picked up the coat with his right hand. 'Could you rip this thing up and make some bandages?'

He tossed the coat at Dehner's head, blocking his eyesight. Dehner stepped sideways, drew his gun, and drilled a shot into Snow's chest. The topside of Slushy Snow's body jolted backwards, then slumped to the ground. A derringer slid from his hand and landed in the dirt.

Rance immediately kicked away the small gun. He looked down at the mining engineer. Feeling for a pulse on the man's neck was only a formality. He knew Slushy Snow was dead.

He suddenly experienced a wave of depression. For the first time he became conscious of a shrill whistle in his ears left by the assault of the gunshots. The whistle elevated to a higher pitch, then his ears were resonating with sharp piercing sounds as if a million worms were slithering about in his head. The worms were singing some morbid song praising death, and praising men who killed other men and provided the worms of the world with succulent meals.

Rance Dehner felt very alone and for a moment he wondered if he could spend his life as a detective: a life lived in a shabby world that often involved killing shabby men.

He inhaled deeply. He had to block out all such thoughts. Self-pity was an indulgence he couldn't allow himself. An innocent man faced a jail sentence and there was a murder to be solved.

The detective began to examine the blood-splattered ground beside the dead body of Slushy Snow. He found a pile of rocks that was obviously man made. Rance tossed the rocks aside until he came to an old coffee can. What Snow had stuffed inside that can could help in the trial which was scheduled for the next day, Dehner thought. He might have found evidence which would help clear Lon Westlake, if only he knew how to use it.

Rance hurried from the mine, mounted his bay and rode back to Slushy Snow's cabin. When he arrived, the worms were no longer dancing in his head.

CHAPTER TWENTY-TWO

Emery Brown and Stacey Hooper were on the porch of the cabin. As he tied his bay to the hitch rail, Dehner asked a question which the grim faces on the two men had already answered. 'You weren't able to save him?'

'Dead,' Brown answered. 'How about Slushy Snow?'

'Same.'

The three men glanced at each other and then glanced at the sky. Dehner realized he couldn't let them drop into a brooding session. 'The man in the moon isn't going to help us.' He stepped quickly onto the porch, 'Come on.'

As they marched inside the cabin, the mood turned more businesslike. A lantern still perched on each side of what was now a corpse. Rance looked carefully at the dead body. 'Emery, does this man resemble Virgil Flynn?'

'Sure does, at first look anyhow. A bit younger than Virgil but, yep, I can see how some folks might think this was Virgil Flynn, what with all his hair cut off and all.'

Dehner crouched over the corpse. 'There are a few small cuts on his head. Whoever shaved it was careless. See that red at the top of his forehead?'

'Blood?' Brown asked.

'I don't think so,' Rance said, 'I bet it's red ink. He couldn't wash it completely off after posing as Virgil.'

The detective buoyed up, walked across the room, and lifted a blanket off Slushy Snow's bed. He spoke again as he placed the blanket over the corpse. 'Stacey, is this the gentleman you were telling me about?'

'Indeed. He looks different with his golden locks gone but that is Willard Fanshaw, known to his family and very small circle of friends as Wild Willie.'

Emery Brown took a few steps away from the man whose life he had tried to save and looked curiously at Hooper. 'I don't know what you're talking about.'

'I do,' Rance snapped, 'but only because Stacey decided to confess before church this morning. I'm sure he'd be happy to also unload his recently troubled past onto you, Emery.'

Rance and Stacey had followed the deputy in stepping away from the corpse. All three men were emotionally drained but realized there was far more work to do.

'Wild Willie inherited his wildness from his father, Bradford,' Stacey explained. 'Mr Bradford Fanshaw had been a decorated soldier in the Confederacy—a fact he referred to often—as well as a successful businessman.'

The deputy's eyes narrowed. 'He must also have been a high stakes gambler, otherwise he'd have never crossed paths with you.'

Stacey appeared mildly impressed by Emery's deduction. 'Correct. Unfortunately, a long night of playing cards could ignite Mr Fanshaw's legendary wildness.'

A smirk crossed Brown's face. 'Bradford Fanshaw accused you of cheating; a gunfight followed and you killed him.'

'Excellent, Deputy! You have proven Rance to be a wise judge of character. He said once we get you away from the beautiful Penelope, you would prove to be a first-rate lawman.'

'Well, this here first-rate lawman doesn't understand how you shooting Bradford Fanshaw led to his son getting himself killed in this cabin.'

Stacey nodded his head and continued his story. 'I gunned down Bradford in a fair fight, of course. Several people witnessed the confrontation and testified that Bradford Fanshaw drew first. As a matter of fact, he had been in several such skirmishes before, only in the past he had been the one left standing with a smoking gun. On the subject of smoke, can I offer you gentlemen a cigar?'

Rance and Emery both shook their heads and then waited patiently as Hooper ignited a stogie. He blew his first cloud of smoke and then returned to his narrative. 'Bradford Fanshaw's wife was long deceased but she had blessed him with two sons. The oldest, Jaime, was a very sensible chap who realized the inevitability of his father dying on a saloon floor. He took no offense, in fact I think he rather relished the notion of being left to the helm of his father's business.'

'But the other son wasn't so agreeable,' Brown said.

'Jaime warned me about his brother. The lad was unbalanced.'

'Unbalanced?' Emery asked.

'He was loony,' Dehner explained.

'And loony in a rather dangerous way,' Stacey fussed with his cigar. 'You see, Willard, or Wild Willie, if you prefer, was determined to avenge his father's death. But Wild Willie didn't care much for direct confrontation. No gunfights for him. He found looking an opponent in the eye to be unnerving and the outcome to be far too uncertain. Wild Willie killed from ambush. His older brother was sure Willard had already killed two men in this manner but his loving father dropped money in the right places and Wild Willie was never charged.'

The deputy pushed his hat back on his head. 'That's why you came to Hard Stone. You figured it was a small, out of the way place. Wild Willie would never find you here and after a while he'd get tired of looking and give up.'

'Yes. Regrettably, it did not turn out that way. Perhaps that is not so regrettable after all. I'm sure you gentlemen will agree with me; it seems unlikely Wild Willie would have reformed and become a useful citizen who encouraged civic pride.'

The deputy threw up both arms in a gesture of resignation. 'But how did Wild Willie end up with a bald head, posing as the ghost of Virgil Flynn?'

'Alas, this is a question I cannot answer. Rance, can you cast more light on this situation?'

'I'm working on it.' The detective glanced backwards to

Willard Fanshaw's corpse. 'I notice that Wild Willie carried a knife on him, a large knife on his belt. I think he was bolder with the knife than he was with a gun.'

Hooper knocked a large ash onto the floor. 'I don't quite follow you.'

'Stacey, have you noticed any changes Slushy Snow made to this cabin since the last time we were here?'

Hooper glanced quickly around him. 'Yes, there is that wretched throw rug: awful-looking old thing and it only covers a comparatively small area. It looks like an ugly patch on an ugly piece of work. Egad, the man even nailed the ugly mess to the floor. It all confirms my suspicion that Slushy Snow was a man with no appreciation for life's finer things.'

'I don't think the rug is there for appearances,' Dehner said.

'What do you mean?' Emery Brown asked.

Rance Dehner took a few quick steps to the rug and gave it a hard yank, ripping it off the nails that had held it to the floor. 'Emery, could you grab one of those lanterns and bring it here?'

The deputy quickly complied with Dehner's request. He then stood holding the light as the three men looked down at the floor.

'Bloodstains!' Brown spoke in an intense, high-pitched voice.

'Yes, I think we are looking at the blood of George Conklin,' Dehner said.

Emery shook his head. 'But ... Conklin's body was found hanging from a tree in the woods right behind the home of Harland Castle.'

'That doesn't mean he was killed there,' Dehner replied.

'I see Rance's point.' Stacey as always seemed amused.

'A man is found hanging from a tree, folks would make the natural assumption that he died from one of several maladies, which could result from being suspended in the air with a rope around your neck. In all likelihood no one inspected the corpse too carefully until Rance did.'

'I think Wild Willie murdered Conklin in this cabin,' Dehner said.

The deputy shook his head a second time. 'I'm not keeping up with you.'

'Some people in Hard Stone have been engaged in a very dangerous charade. Willard Fanshaw was a part of that charade. But, of course, he had to be kept hidden most of the time. This cabin was the perfect hideout. Everyone knew Slushy Snow was obsessed with his privacy and they left him alone. They were going to keep Willard hidden here until they didn't need him anymore.'

Emery took off his hat and ran a hand through his hair. 'So, how did George Conklin end up getting killed here?'

Dehner explained: 'Conklin broke into this cabin. Wild Willie thought he had to kill the banker, otherwise Conklin could destroy the whole charade. The body was then hung from a tree and made a part of the ghost of Virgil Flynn's next appearance.'

Brown let out a long sigh. 'But how did George Conklin get into this place?'

'Stacey was right. Most people didn't give George Conklin's body much attention but I did. I checked his pants pockets and found this.' The detective pulled out a shiny gold-colored object.

'That's a right fancy key,' Emery said.

'And I believe it fits a right fancy lock.' Dehner walked over to the cabin's door and, using the key, opened the lock that hung on the door handle. 'Somehow, George Conklin had a key to this cabin.'

The other two men had followed Rance to the door. Emery Brown looked totally confused, 'So, why did Conklin come here?'

'I don't know,' Dehner admitted.

'Rance, earlier you made a statement that rather intrigued me.' Stacey blew a cloud of cigar smoke before continuing. 'You said some people in Hard Stone are engaged in a dangerous charade. Exactly who are these people?'

'I'm afraid that is another question I can't answer … not for sure. I don't have any proof.'

'And tomorrow is Lon Westlake's trial,' Brown added.

Stacey Hooper pointed toward the ceiling with his stogie and proclaimed, 'In a trial one must always provide proof!'

'Maybe,' Rance said. 'Maybe….'

CHAPTER TWENTY-THREE

Rance Dehner felt ridiculous and scared. He was seated at the table for the defense directly beside his client, Lon Westlake. For Lon's sake, Dehner tried not to appear nervous. But he kept recalling the fact that his formal education had stopped at the eighth grade. He had never even been near a college.

Of course, a college graduate would not be all that impressed with Rance's surroundings. The trial was being held in the Lucky Miner Saloon. The circuit judge would preside at a battered table which sat in front of the bar. A gavel and a Bible lay on the table. To Dehner's left stood twelve empty chairs which would be filled with members of the jury who had not yet been selected.

The saloon's round tables were stacked against the side walls. Twelve rows of chairs blanketed a large portion of the saloon. An informal aisle divided the rows with seven chairs on each side, and all of them were filled. A lot of children were present, many of them punching each other and indulging in horseplay. The adults weren't much better as they swapped jokes and laughed loudly. The mood was festive.

The area around Rance Dehner provided a patch of solemnity. Lon Westlake appeared stoic but worried. Immediately behind Lon sat Penelope Castle and her father. They both looked grim as did Ralph Morris, the man who worked as a clerk at Westlake's General Store. Only Stacey Hooper, who sat directly behind Dehner, beamed a confident smile.

Rance wanted to provide some distraction for his client. He spoke in a low voice to Westlake. 'What can you tell me about Whittaker Stanton, the prosecuting attorney? I know he is Hard Stone's only lawyer but my knowledge of the man ends there.'

Lon glanced to his right where Stanton was sitting by himself at the prosecutor's table intensely reading some papers, or pretending to. The attorney was thin, almost frail-looking with a soft chin, a large forehead, and brown hair carefully arranged to cover a bald spot. He appeared to be somewhere in his forties.

Westlake looked back at Dehner. 'Whittaker Stanton is a terrific speaker. He comes from Boston. Rumor goes he wanted to be an actor but his family is very prominent and they forbade it. I think one reason he left Boston is because he couldn't get along with his family. He seems to be a very bitter man.'

'Does he drink much?' Dehner asked.

'Yes,' Westlake answered. 'And when he gets drunk he says some very ugly things about people.'

'That could be another reason he left Boston,' Dehner replied.

The detective took one last quick glance around the saloon. Emery Brown was standing in the back. Earlier that morning, Dehner had asked a favor of the deputy. Brown had reluctantly agreed.

Rance Dehner also noted that the near riot at the church the previous day had not been forgotten. Most of the men were wearing guns, including the man in charge of the defense.

'Quiet everyone!' Sheriff Kendall yelled as he stepped in front of the judge's table. 'This here court is now in session, circuit judge Lawrence Buchanan presiding. All rise!'

As Kendall stepped back, a short, barrel-chested man with thick white hair that rimmed his collar stepped to the front and proclaimed, 'You may be seated!'

Chair legs rubbing against the floor resounded over the saloon for a moment, the circuit judge waited for quiet before continuing, 'I remind you folks that it makes not a whit of difference what the Lucky Miner is most o' the time. Right now, it's a court o' law and all o' ya had better act accordingly.' Buchanan looked around the room. 'I notice we got a lotta young folks on hand.' His eyes rested on an older, neatly dressed woman who was the town's school-marm. 'Mrs Stanfield, you have anything to do with this?'

'Yes, Lawrence, I mean Your Honor, I do. School is, of course, out for the summer. But I encouraged all the families in Hard Stone to allow their young 'uns to watch the trial. I want them to see our legal system in action. When they return to the classroom in the fall, I'm having them write an essay on what they witness here today.'

Buchanan looked displeased but resigned. 'Well, I suppose that beats having 'em write on, "How I Spent My Summer".' His eyes performed a blistering survey of the children. 'As an officer o' the court, I expect you children to conduct yourselves like grown-ups.' The judge paused, as if wondering whether the grown-ups really provided all that good a model. He then plowed on. 'If any o' ya act up I'll have ya removed from the court and I'll tell your folks to give ya a spanking where ya won't sit down for a week. So, behave yourselves!'

Silence covered the Lucky Miner. The adults seemed as intimidated by Lawrence Buchanan as the children. The judge walked behind his desk but remained standing. 'Our first order o' business is ta choose a jury. Every man who serves on the jury must work and vote in this town—no saddlebums. What's more, nobody who has a prejudice in this case can serve on the jury. Now, let me explain what that means.'

Judge Buchanan pointed at a man sitting in the third row. 'Edward McNelty, I recall the last time I was in Hard Stone, Lon Westlake threw ya outta his store because ya were drunk, cussing up a storm in front o' ladies and acting ornery. That makes you prejudiced!'

'Ah, Judge, Westlake threw me outta his store lots of times, ' McNelty replied. 'That don't bother me none, it sure don't make me preje ... you know.'

'I know you can't be on the jury,' Buchanan yelled accusingly.

The judge cleared his throat before continuing. 'There's another side ta this prejudice thing. I know Lon Westlake has extended credit ta a lotta people in Hard Stone. Naturally, they're grateful and that disqualifies them from being on the jury. Don't any o' ya who feel beholden to Lon try ta get on the jury. I'll question ya and I'll find ya out. You'll be under oath meaning ya can go to jail for telling a lie.'

The judge sat down and the proceedings began. Jury selection took about forty-five minutes. The twelve men ranged from local businessmen to miners and cowboys. They all looked pleased to be in a position to determine whether one of their local citizens went free or spent the next twenty years of his life in the hell of prison. Rance Dehner wasn't sure what to make of that.

'Mr Stanton, you may now get us started.'

'Thank you, Your Honor.' Whittaker Stanton sprang up from his chair and strode toward the jury. Dehner recalled what his client had told him about Stanton's desire to be in the theater. He did look like an actor prancing onto the stage. He was dressed in a dark blue suit with a thin, black bow tie. He was one of the few men in the room not wearing a gun.

'Gentlemen, today we find ourselves in an extraordinary situation which, I believe, is unprecedented in the annals of law!'

Dehner watched the faces of the jury members. They might not have completely understood Stanton's opening remark but they were impressed. Their eyes were wide and a few mouths hung open.

Whittaker Stanton had started strong and didn't intend to let up. 'Hard Stone is a town in mourning. I'm sure all of you are familiar with a Mr Sydney Snow.' Whittaker paused and smiled benignly, 'A man known affectionately as Slushy Snow. Mr Snow, a brilliant mining engineer, rescued this town from total ruin when he discovered a rich vein in an old mine most people had thought was played out.

'And, as fate would have it, Slushy Snow did even more for this town. On that horrible night when our bank was robbed, Mr Snow saw Lon Westlake committing the heinous crime. He wanted to testify to that fact at this trial. But, as you gentlemen know, that opportunity was violently snatched from him.'

Stanton took a few dramatic strides which left him in front of the defense table. 'Last night, the dead body of Sydney Snow was found at the mining site by Sheriff Pete Kendall and Horst Weber, the guard at the mine. Mr Snow had been shot twice. And gentlemen, we know the identity of the man who took the life of our good friend, Slushy Snow.'

Whittaker slowly lifted one arm into the air and with his index finger serving as a pointer, thrust it in Dehner's direction. 'The man who put two bullets into Slushy Snow is the very man who is serving as Lon Westlake's defense attorney. The man who has admitted to killing the one eye witness to the bank hold-up calls himself a detective. Detective! Gentlemen, I submit to you that *detective* is just a fancy word for gunslinger.'

Stanton dropped his arm and slowly strolled back in the direction of the jury. 'I am a man who has dedicated himself to the law. Sheriff Kendall hasn't charged Rance Dehner with any crime ... not yet anyway. Therefore, Mr Dehner has a right to take part in this trial today, but his words will not stand against the chief witness for the prosecution.'

The prosecutor pressed his lips together as if

momentarily holding back an astonishing revelation. When he spoke his voice sounded almost mystical. 'Sydney Snow, a man beloved by this community, who was buried in Hard Stone only a couple of hours ago will, this afternoon, speak to us from the grave!'

The jury members appeared to lean back in their chairs as Stanton eyed them ferociously. 'Sheriff Kendall will testify before you that Sydney Snow identified the man who robbed the bank and rode quickly out of town; the man who buried the money somewhere and then returned to Hard Stone. What's more, the prosecution will present a document written by Mr Snow where he states in his own words what he witnessed the night of the hold-up. Yes, gentlemen, today Mr Snow will speak to us from the grave and identify the bank robber as … ' Whittaker Stanton suddenly turned and faced the defense table, 'Lon Westlake!'

As Whittaker walked majestically back to his chair, a scattering of applause skidded across the Lucky Miner. 'You're right,' Rance whispered to his client, 'Mr Stanton is a very good speaker.'

'Mr Dehner, are you ready?' the judge asked.

Dehner didn't really know the answer to that question but he tried to look confident as he stood up. 'Yes, Your Honor, the defense is ready.'

CHAPTER TWENTY-FOUR

Rance approached the jury slowly. 'You men just heard Mr Stanton claim a detective is nothing more than a gunfighter.

I'll allow all of you to make your own judgments on that statement.

'But there is something about a detective's life you may not know. I spend a lot of time alone, which means I read a lot. Books are often my only companions. Oh sure, I have a good horse, but he's not much of a conversationalist.'

A few guffaws sounded from the jurors and the spectators. Rance hoped he had destroyed or at least wounded the notion that he was a gunslick who had purposely killed the prosecution's main witness.

He continued in a conversational manner. 'I've read a lot of William Shakespeare, perhaps some of you men have, too. Oh, many folks think Shakespeare is high hat but let me tell you he can be pretty funny at times, just like Mark Twain.'

He studied the jurors as he spoke. He had their attention, but they were not mesmerized as they had been by the prosecutor. For a moment, he wondered if he should copy the dramatics of Whittaker Stanton. He quickly rejected the notion. Stacey Hooper was right: his acting skills were severely limited.

'Yep, Shakespeare can be funny,' Dehner continued, 'but he is most famous for his tragedies. *Tragedy*. That is a very sad word. A tragedy occurs when a good man is brought down by a flaw in his character. School teachers like Mrs Stanfield sometimes refer to this as the fatal flaw.'

The detective quickly shifted his gaze to the spectators. His words were making one of them nervously twitch. Good.

Dehner looked back at the jury. 'Gentlemen, the story the defense will present to you today is a tragedy. It will be a story of good men gone terribly wrong and finding themselves having to cover up the brutal murder of George

Conklin. And, I'm afraid, this tragedy will impact every man, woman, and child in Hard Stone. Your lives will not be the same. Thank you.'

There was no applause as Rance returned to his place at the defense table. A feeling of uneasiness seemed to have afflicted the crowd. No one wanted to be part of a tragedy.

The detective noted his client didn't look too happy. Lon obviously felt Rance Dehner had been whipped good by Whittaker Stanton. Penelope Castle appeared to share her fiancé's opinion.

Only Stacey Hooper seemed pleased by Dehner's opening statement. He leaned forward and whispered to Rance, 'Superb performance; the references to Shakespeare put you far ahead of your opponent. You are elevating this trial to a higher level, bringing culture to the masses.'

Hooper's statement did nothing to make Lon or Penelope feel any better.

Curiosity danced in the eyes of Judge Lawrence Buchanan. He obviously believed Dehner was up to something but had no idea what. His voice sounded even more caustic than usual when he addressed the prosecutor. 'You may call your first witness, Mr Stanton.'

'Thank you, Your Honor. I call to the stand, Sheriff Pete Kendall.'

Sheriff Kendall stepped forward and placed his right hand on the Bible. He said 'I do' to the oath hastily recited by Buchanan. The judge nodded to a chair directly beside him, 'Be seated.'

As Dehner listened to Whittaker Stanton examine his witness he realized Stanton was both a superb actor and a competent lawyer. Stanton had the sheriff review the events of the night the bank was held up. Kendall testified he and

Emery Brown were dealing with a problem at the Red Dog Saloon when George Conklin and Slushy Snow rushed into the place with news that the bank had been robbed. Snow identified Lon Westlake as the thief. Conklin and Snow had burned up a fair amount of time finding the lawmen. So, the sheriff and his deputy headed for Westlake's home. They found Westlake there. His horse was in a corral at the back of the house. The horse had been ridden hard.

The prosecutor made a quizzical face and asked Kendall a question the two men had rehearsed in advance. 'Sheriff, didn't it impress you as unusual that Lon Westlake chose to remain in Hard Stone, instead of riding off with the money?'

'No, Mr Stanton, there was nothing odd about it.'

'Please explain why.'

'Westlake has lived in this town for years. If he were to disappear after the robbery the whole town woulda knowed he did it. Every lawman within miles would be hunting him.'

'And, Sheriff Kendall, could you give us your theory as to what the defendant did with the money?'

'It's pretty obvious. He buried the money outside of town, planned to get it later.'

Stacey Hooper again whispered to Dehner. 'I think you should object. What the sheriff just said was hearsay.'

'Kendall has already expressed his theory in the newspaper, everyone on the jury knows it,' Dehner whispered back. 'Besides, I can't be picky. What I have planned is not exactly in line with legal procedure.'

Whittaker Stanton was moving to a different line of questioning. 'Sheriff, after you arrested Lon Westlake, did you take any action in regard to the man we all knew as Slushy Snow?'

'Yes, I had him write out what he had witnessed that

night on a piece of paper and sign it. I also signed the paper. I believe you lawyers call it an affidavit.'

'You are absolutely right, Mr Kendall.' Whittaker's face beamed approval of the sheriff's legal knowledge. Dehner could hear Stacey Hooper groaning.

The lawyer dramatically stepped over to the prosecutor's table, lifted a piece of paper from it, and returned to his witness. 'Sheriff, is this the affidavit you and Mr Snow signed that fateful night?'

'Yep.'

Holding the affidavit high in his right hand, Stanton strode toward the jury. 'As I promised you, gentlemen, Slushy Snow is speaking to us today from the grave. Here in his own words you will find Mr Snow backing up everything Sheriff Pete Kendall has just testified to. Read for yourselves the words of this man who did so much for our town.'

Whittaker handed the paper to the jury foreman. Several jury members looked over the foreman's shoulder as he read the document. The affidavit was then passed off to the remaining jury members. Whittaker Stanton stood by in a stoic manner until everyone on the jury had read the document and the foreman handed it back to him. He then paraded to the judge's desk and, in an almost courtly bow, handed the document to Judge Buchanan.

'Exhibit A, Your Honor.'

Lawrence Buchanan looked toward the defense table. 'Do you wish to examine the affidavit, Mr Dehner?'

'No thank you, Your Honor, that will not be necessary.'

Whittaker Stanton smirked as if his opponent had just formally surrendered. 'I have no further questions for Sheriff Kendall, Your Honor.'

'Do you wish to cross examine, Mr Dehner?'

'Yes, Your Honor, I have just a few questions.' Rance spoke casually as if he were about to clear up a few minor details. He approached the defendant in a casual manner.

'Sheriff, I have had some conversations with your deputy, Emery Brown. Mr Brown tells me that, most of the time, one of you tries to handle trouble on his own while the other stays in the office, in the event something else comes up. Is that correct?'

Kendall sensed where this was going and tried to cut it off quick. 'We can't do it that way always, sometimes both of us has gotta look into it.'

'Of course,' Dehner kept the mood informal. 'So, the situation at the Red Dog was a dangerous one: a situation which demanded the attention of both of Hard Stone's lawmen?'

'Well … no … but it seemed that way at the start.'

'When did you first realize there was trouble at the Red Dog?'

'I was outside the office, just getting back from doing a round and I heard loud voices coming from the Red Dog Saloon: two jaspers shouting at each other. They sounded plenty angry. I opened the office door and called out to Deputy Brown. The two of us headed to the Red Dog.'

Dehner gave both the jury and the spectators a lopsided smile, before asking his next question. 'Is the sheriff of Hard Stone unable to handle an argument between two men in a saloon all by himself?'

Whittaker Stanton stood up. 'Your Honor, I object. Mr Dehner is attacking the judgment and character of a man who has served nobly as this town's sheriff for over twenty years.'

Rance maintained a smile. 'I'll withdraw the question, Your Honor. Sheriff Kendall, could you tell me approximately how long you and Emery Brown were in the Red Dog Saloon that night before Mr Snow and Mr Conklin arrived to inform you of the bank robbery?'

'No, Mr Dehner, I can't! I didn't have the leisure to check my pocket watch.'

'Deputy Brown informed me that the trouble at the Red Dog was very minor. In fact, there was really no serious trouble at all, is that correct?'

'Yes.'

'He also told me the two of you remained in the saloon. You encouraged him to stay and just talk with the owner and customers, is that also correct?'

'A lawman can't be standoffish. You gotta know the people in your town. It's important to spend time jawing with folks now and again.'

'Of course.' A trace of skepticism entered Dehner's voice. 'George Conklin and Slushy Snow found you in the Red Dog after spending a lot of time looking for you elsewhere. They told you about the bank hold-up. You and Emery Brown headed for Lon Westlake's home. When you got there Deputy Brown knocked on the front door while you checked the horse in Westlake's corral. The Appaloosa had been ridden hard, correct?'

'Yes.'

'Did Deputy Brown check the horse?'

'No. There was no reason for him to!'

'The next morning you took Westlake's horse to Barton's Livery?'

'Yes.'

Borrowing a touch of Stanton's techniques, Dehner gave a theatrical laugh. 'You made Rufus Barton angry didn't you, Sheriff?'

'I don't know what you're talking about.'

'Mr Barton told me you brought him the Appaloosa at the most busy time of his day. It was an hour or so before he could care for the horse.'

'I got a lot to do myself, Mr Dehner. I can't always oblige the schedule of other people.'

'Sheriff, you took that horse to the livery at a time when you knew Barton couldn't give it his attention and when he could, he'd still be in a hectic time of day and unlikely to remember much about Lon Westlake's horse. You did that for the same reason you made sure Emery Brown didn't see the horse, because you lied, didn't you, Pete Kendall. Lon's horse hadn't been ridden at all on the night of the bank robbery?!'

A loud roar ignited in the saloon. Kendall shouted that Dehner was the liar while Whittaker Stanton sprang to his feet with angry objections. Several spectators were yelling loudly, their voices colliding into a loud explosion of sound.

Lawrence Buchanan pounded his gavel on the old desk. At first, the pounding only added to the noise resounding through the Lucky Miner Saloon, but the judge's booming demands of 'Order!' eventually began to diminish the racket.

As soon as his voice could be heard, Dehner addressed the bench. 'Your Honor, I withdraw my question and have no further questions for Sheriff Kendall.'

'The witness may step down.' The judge watched carefully as Pete Kendall left the chair and slowly passed by the defense table, giving Dehner a threatening glare.

Buchanan turned his eyes to the prosecutor. 'Mr Stanton, do you wish to call another witness?'

Willard Stanton rose and stood behind the prosecutor's table, striking a majestic pose. Although he technically addressed the judge, his eyes were fixed on the jury. 'No, Your Honor, there is no need to call any more witnesses. The testimonies of Sydney Snow and Sheriff Pete Kendall are all that are needed to ascertain what happened on the night the bank was robbed. No reprehensible attacks on the character of Hard Stone's fine sheriff, made by an outsider to our town, can blind our good citizens to the truth.'

A smug smile covered Stanton's face as he sat down. The lawyer obviously believed he had his case won. Dehner could tell by the wan expression on Lon Westlake's face that his client believed Whittaker could well be right.

'Mr Dehner, you may call your first witness.'

'Your Honor, I call Harland Castle.'

As a surprised Harland Castle clumsily made his way to the judge's table and took the oath, Rance's eyes briefly fused with those of Penelope. She looked concerned and angry, obviously believing Dehner should have given her father advance notice that he would be called to the stand.

Harland's nervousness subsided as he sat in the witness chair. He obviously saw the comforting looks he received from the spectators.

'Mr Castle, as the prosecutor has informed the court, I am a detective. In my job as a detective I have been asking some of the citizens of Hard Stone a lot of questions. I have learned some interesting things about you. Your father was a miner, is that correct?'

'Yes,' Harland replied.

'And after a year or two of working in the mines yourself, you moved to Hard Stone and began your own mining company. Is that also correct?'

'Yes. I was very blessed. I was able to find investors to back up Castle Mining Operations.'

Dehner continued to encourage his witness. 'You did a lot more than just start what became a very successful company in Hard Stone, Mr Castle. You practically built this town. You have a well-deserved reputation for helping people in need. And your generosity does not stop at helping individuals. You're responsible for starting a school in Hard Stone.'

Castle smiled as he replied. 'A lot of different types become miners. There are young men seeking adventure and fortune. They don't stay around too long. But there are also family men. Men with children who need to be taught how to read, write, and do arithmetic. I started the school for them and for myself too. I had a daughter who needed book learning. Penelope caused Mrs Stanfield some frustration, but I think she turned out well.'

There was a sprinkling of laughter in the Lucky Miner. Dehner waited for it to subside. 'You also had a hand in establishing a church in Hard Stone, Mr Castle. Is that correct?'

'Yes.'

'And you also became good friends with one of your miners, Jess Nevin, the brother of Reverend Thorton Nevin?'

'Yes. Jess Nevin wanted to follow in my footsteps and eventually move into the business side of mining. He had great potential. I made him a foreman. Through our friendship I learned Jess's brother was a preacher.'

'I would reckon that Jess Nevin was a comfort to you when your wife died?'

Whittaker Stanton rose to his feet. 'Your Honor, I have tried to be patient with Mr Dehner. I realize he has no training in the law. He is also an outsider to Hard Stone and knows nothing about the town. But the man is wasting our time. All of us gathered here today are aware of the marvelous contributions Harland Castle has made to Hard Stone. We don't need a history lesson from Mr Rance Dehner. And there is no reason for this outsider to dig up painful memories and throw them in the face of one of our town's most distinguished citizens!'

The judge's eyes looked harsh. 'The prosecutor has a point, Mr Dehner! Is all this background stuff taking us anywhere?'

The murmuring that spread across the saloon was quickly aborted by Lawrence Buchanan's gavel. But it lasted long enough for Dehner to understand the crowd was not on his side.

'Yes, Your Honor,' Rance said. 'I am moving toward a very important set of facts.'

'Well move quickly!' The judge's demeanor became friendly as he addressed Harland Castle. 'You may answer the question.'

'Jess Nevin was a good friend and, of course, a comfort to me when my wife died.'

'And it must have been very hard on you when Jess Nevin was killed in the mine explosion?'

'Yes.'

Dehner paused. Lawrence Buchanan's eyes flared with hostility. The detective could sense the anger building against him from the crowd. 'You must have felt very alone and miserable when you learned the mine was almost played out.'

Harland rubbed his hands together as if he were cold. 'Yes, of course, but then I thought about getting another opinion. I decided to call in—'

Dehner cut off his witness. 'The time for lies is over, Mr Castle! You've been in mining all of your life! You didn't need Slushy Snow to tell you anything. The whole story about a new vein being found in the old mine was a hoax. A hoax that ended in murder!'

Angry shouts fired from across the saloon. The anger was directed at Rance Dehner. Whittaker Stanton sprang to his feet and waited until the judge had gaveled the noise down. 'Your Honor, the conduct of Mr Rance Dehner is outrageous. I respectfully demand he be removed as counsel for the defense!'

Lawrence Buchanan pointed the gavel at Dehner as if it were a six-gun. 'Dehner, ya have exhausted my patience and the patience of everyone else in this building. I am hereby declaring a mistrial. For your own good ya had better ride outta Hard Stone fast—'

'He's telling the truth.'

The voice was so soft, it startled the judge. Buchanan stopped speaking, was quiet for a moment, then looked at the man sitting beside him. 'What did ya say, Harland?'

'It's true. God help me. Everything Rance Dehner just said is true.'

CHAPTER TWENTY-FIVE

A tense quiet enveloped the Lucky Miner. Dehner spoke gently. 'Thank you for that admission, Mr Castle. I know how difficult it was. But it's time for the whole story to come out. You'll have to answer some more questions.'

'Yes … go ahead.'

'Like I said before, you built Hard Stone. For years, you were the man people could go to with a problem. You fixed things. But when you discovered the mine was about played out there was nothing you could do.'

Harland Castle's eyes were down and his face ashen. He could no longer face his fellow townsmen. 'Hard Stone was doomed, a town I had given my whole life to … the two people I could talk things over with in the past, my wife and Jess Nevin, were both dead.'

'It goes further than that, doesn't it, Mr Castle? Years of generosity to others have left your own financial situation precarious.'

'Yes. I was confused, didn't know where to turn.'

'You had known Sheriff Pete Kendall for twenty years. You ended up confiding in him about the mine.'

'The worse mistake of my life,' Castle said.

Dehner quickly eyed Kendall, who was sitting at the far end of a row of chairs behind the prosecutor's table, near a side wall. Hatred flamed in his eyes and his body was rigid, like a wild animal getting ready to strike. Rance looked once again at the witness. 'Could you explain what you meant by the last statement, Mr Castle?'

'When I told Kendall about the mine, he came up with the idea of claiming there was a rich new vein in the closed mine.'

'But before closing that mine, Mr Castle, you had told everyone the mine was played out.'

Castle nodded his head. 'Yes, Kendall said there was an easy way around that. We'd bring in a professional mining engineer, talk him up as being a genius; the engineer would discover this new vein.'

'And I'll bet Sheriff Kendall knew just the man for the job.'

'Yes, the man everyone called Slushy Snow.'

'And the sheriff was certain Slushy Snow would go along with the scheme?'

'For a price. Snow was a gambler as well as an engineer. He owed almost four thousand dollars to a very violent man. He demanded we pay him five thousand to go along with the scheme. He wanted some money to keep for himself.'

'And where did you get the money to pay Slushy Snow?'

'I think you know the answer to the question, Mr Dehner.'

'You had to bring George Conklin in on the plan. He arranged a phony bank robbery, claiming ten thousand dollars had been stolen. In fact, five thousand went to Snow; you three men split up what was left.'

'Yes.'

'Mr Castle, what was the purpose behind this deception?'

Harland Castle turned his head away and yanked a handkerchief from his coat pocket. Dehner paused in his questioning and quickly scanned the makeshift courtroom. He noted that Penelope Castle was now sitting beside Lon Westlake at the defense table. He had his arm around her.

Harland put his handkerchief away and looked at Dehner. 'I apologize for—'

'No need to apologize, please continue.'

Harland Castle's voice was now firm. 'Both Kendall and I thought Reverend Thorton Nevin was a bit crazy and, of course, everyone in Hard Stone knows Tom Flynn is ... well ... they know what he's like. Both men have brothers buried in the old mine. We thought they would go crazy when they learned the mine was to be reopened. We hoped Reverend

Nevin would try to organize the church against the mine reopening.'

'Why?' Dehner asked.

'The main investors in Castle Mining Operations are two big city fools from San Francisco. I would offer to sell the mine to them at a good price. They would think I couldn't stand the heat from the church folks and grab at the offer without asking questions or taking a careful look at the mine.'

'Why did you frame Lon Westlake for the hold-up?'

'We had to frame someone. The bank is owned by the Westward Bank of Commerce. They wield a lot of influence. If someone didn't get arrested for the hold-up, US marshals would be all over this area investigating the robbery and trying to recover the money.'

Dehner put force into his voice. 'Lon Westlake was an easy man to frame. Almost the whole town knows his schedule. The law would be content to keep an eye on Lon after he got out of jail and wait for the day when he goes to dig up the money. You were willing to send an innocent man to prison, a man your daughter loves.'

'No!' Harland shouted. 'That wasn't how it was!'

'Then how was it?'

'Our original plan was to have Slushy Snow act confused on the witness stand. His testimony would be worthless and therefore the jury would have to find Lon innocent. By then, the trail would be cold and the law would be less aggressive.'

'And the folks at the bank and the law would think Lon was guilty and got off because one man stumbled over his testimony.'

'Yes.' For the first time since his admission, Harland

Castle raised his eyes and looked directly at Lon Westlake. 'I'm sorry, Lon. I'm sorry....'

Westlake's face reflected sympathy. 'It's OK, Mr Castle. Everything is going to be fine.'

Penelope Castle stared at her father. Rance couldn't tell what was in her eyes but it wasn't sympathy. Harland Castle realized the same thing and knew Lon Westlake was wrong. For Harland, nothing would be fine again. Ever.

Dehner continued, 'So, Mr Castle, did this plan work? Were the townspeople outraged by the mine being reopened?'

'No, not at first. I underestimated Reverend Nevin. Tom acted crazy but the reverend kept him in check.'

'But you were soon to have help, Mr Castle.' Dehner looked at Judge Buchanan who seemed to be in a state of shock. 'Your Honor, I have no further questions for Mr Castle. I would like to call Mr Stacey Hooper to the stand.'

Buchanan turned to the witness. 'Ya can step down.'

Harland Castle's body trembled as he spoke to the judge. 'I'm sorry, Lawrence.'

Lawrence Buchanan pressed his lips together before speaking. 'So am I, Harland.'

For a moment the founder of Castle Mining Operations gripped the arms of his chair as if he didn't want to leave it and encounter the harsh reality that awaited him. He slowly lifted himself up and walked back to his seat. The eyes of almost everyone in the Lucky Miner watched him in near silence. Harland's clumsy footsteps sounded eerie: the sounds of a death rattle.

The mine owner stopped at the defense table and looked at his daughter. Penelope stared at her father as if beholding a stranger, then looked away. Harland took his seat in the row behind the defense table and once again looked at his daughter. He saw only the back of her head.

As soon as Harland had returned to his chair, Stacey Hooper shot up and strutted forward. As he approached the judge's desk, he smiled at the spectators and gave a quick wave.

Judge Buchanan was not amused. 'Mr Hooper, I will remind you that this is still a court of law. Place your right hand on the Good Book.'

'Of course, Your Honor,' Stacey proclaimed. 'This is quite an experience for me—the first time in my life I have ever touched a Bible.'

Laughter exploded in the courtroom. Even Lawrence Buchanan smiled. Dehner realized the laughter was providing an emotional release. A tragedy needs comedy relief, he thought to himself.

Stacey Hooper was the man to provide that relief. Under questioning from Rance, Hooper explained how after killing a man in a 'duel of honor' he had become a target for the man's son. 'Willard Fanshaw, better known as Wild Willie, a man of low morals and even lower mental aptitude; he is totally depraved. He kills men by ambush.'

Dehner had his friend explain how the two of them had been shot at while returning from interviewing Slushy Snow. 'But that ambush ended rather strangely, didn't it, Mr Hooper.'

'Indeed, our ambusher suddenly stopped shooting at us, as if he had a pressing engagement elsewhere.'

'Do you recall hearing voices from the top of the hill, as if someone were talking to the man who was trying to kill us?'

'Yes. Both men employed profanity. I wouldn't want

to quote them directly and lower the tone of this august assemblage.'

'I have no further questions, Mr Hooper, thank you. Your Honor, I would like to call to the stand, Sheriff Pete Kendall.'

The judge scratched his head before speaking. 'The purpose o' this trial was ta establish the guilt or innocence o' Lon Westlake in regard ta the bank robbery. We've pretty well done that. But I would sure like to know exactly what's been going on in this town and I think everyone here feels the same. Mr Stanton, does the prosecution, which at this point has nothing left ta do, have any objection ta Mr Dehner continuing?'

Whittaker Stanton shook his head and waved his hand as if shooing off a pesky insect. The frustrated actor now wanted to be invisible.

'Pete Kendall, take the stand,' Buchanan said.

Kendall approached the judge's table laconically, and smiled as he was reminded he was still under oath. Dehner had no idea what the disgraced sheriff's plan was at this point but he was certain Kendall had a plan of some kind.

Rance decided to match the lawman's mock good nature. 'Sheriff, before I begin my questions, I have a confession to make. This morning, I asked your deputy to break the law.'

Nervous laughter bounced about the Lucky Miner. Dehner continued: 'Emery Brown broke into your house this morning when you thought he was doing a round. Deputy Brown discovered close to three thousand dollars in cash!'

An angry shout exploded from somewhere in the room. 'You're a cheat and a liar, Kendall, and we all trusted you!' Similar cries began to fill the Lucky Miner and Buchanan had to once again pound his gavel.

Dehner realized he was playing with emotional dyna-mite. Hard Stone was doomed and everyone in the room now realized it. Their livelihoods were gone. He was in the midst of people whose souls had just taken a vicious hit. They wanted to strike out at something or someone.

He addressed his witness. 'I told you about Emery's find, Sheriff Kendall, because I want you to know there is little reason for you to continue with the deception you tried to foist onto this town.'

A bland smile played across Kendall's face but the hatred was still in his eyes. 'Of course, Mr Dehner. I'm just a small town lawdog, shoulda knowed better than to try to fool a smart detective like you.'

'When did you first notice Willard Fanshaw?' Dehner asked.

'Shortly after he rode into town. That's one of those little things a small town lawdog does, he watches for strangers.'

'And Sheriff, did you notice that Fanshaw bore some resemblance to Virgil Flynn, one of the two men who remains buried in the old mine?'

'Yep, Mr Detective, you see we old star packers are used to reading wanted circulars. Of course, outlaws are always growing beards or shaving them off, that sorta thing. I had no trouble imagining Fanshaw with no hair and a cut on his forehead.'

'Did you notice anything strange in Fanshaw's behavior?'

'Sure did, he was following you and Stacey Hooper. Too bad you didn't notice that yourself, Mr Detective.'

'And you followed Willard Fanshaw when he followed Stacey Hooper and me out to Slushy Snow's cabin?'

'Yep.'

'And you saw Willard Fanshaw attempt to ambush us?'

'Sure did. He woulda killed you both if I hadn't stopped him.'

'You stopped Fanshaw and brought him into town. You had in mind an idea to make the original plan you cooked up work, didn't you, Sheriff Kendall?'

Kendall nodded his head. 'Fanshaw wanted to kill Hooper. I promised I'd help him do just that and give him a hundred dollars to boot. But first he had to do me a little favor. I cut the guy's hair off and put some red ink on his forehead. I knew Tom Flynn cleaned the church every night. I figured an appearance by his brother Virgil would put Tom and the good reverend in a real crazy mood. And that's what happened.'

'Pretty clever notion, Sheriff, but there was a problem. You couldn't have Willard Fanshaw walking around town during the day, so you hid him out at Slushy Snow's cabin.'

Kendall barked out a harsh laugh. 'Perfect hideout. Everyone knowed Slushy Snow was a real private man ... spending all his time with maps of the new vein that was gonna save the town.'

'Did you tell Harland Castle and George Conklin about this development, about the ghost of Virgil Flynn appearing to Reverend Nevin and Tom?'

'Told Castle, not Conklin.'

'Why did you leave the banker out?'

'George Conklin was already a nervous Nellie. I didn't think he could handle it.'

'You were right, Sheriff, and I made Conklin even more nervous. I told him, truthfully, that the Westward Bank had hired the agency I work for to investigate the robbery.'

Dehner paused and began to pace up and down in front

of his witness. As he spoke his eyes shifted back and forth between the lawman and the spectators. 'The way I see it, George Conklin panicked. He decided to make a run for it, probably was going to head for Mexico. But first, he wanted to grab some more money. He assumed Slushy Snow had hidden the remaining thousand dollars he had somewhere in his cabin. He broke into the cabin while Snow was at the mine.

'Slushy Snow wasn't there, but Willard Fanshaw was. Fanshaw stabbed Conklin to death. Snow returned to a very gruesome sight in his cabin. He brought the problem to you, didn't he, Sheriff?'

Kendall laughed and shrugged his shoulders. 'You know, it wasn't as big a problem as you might think. We had planned on having Virgil's ghost make one more appearance—at the home of Harland Castle. Everyone in Hard Stone would take the word of the Castles! Harland told me he could convince his daughter about the ghost.'

Penelope Castle turned her head and glared at her father. Harland bowed his head and looked at the floor.

Pete Kendall continued: 'Slushy and me tied Conklin's body to a tree in the woods right behind Harland's house. We had to keep it in Slushy's place for a while, of course. Couldn't hang it in the tree right away, otherwise the coyotes would have gotten to George before we could carry out the scheme.'

'Poor George Conklin!' Dehner shouted those words. 'He was wrong about the money being in Slushy's cabin. Snow kept it hidden in the old mine. And after you learned George was dead you stole his cut of the money from his house.'

'Figured George wouldn't be needing it anymore.'

Dehner stopped pacing and looked at the judge. 'Your Honor, I have no further questions for this witness.'

'Thank you, Mr Dehner. The witness *will not* step down.' Buchanan motioned toward Emery Brown. 'Deputy, will you come forward please.'

His face the color of water, Emery made quick strides to the front and stood beside Pete Kendall, who was still seated. The sheriff nodded at his deputy, who nodded back. Dehner was now standing on the other side of the judge's desk.

The judge's voice resounded with an intense anger. 'Deputy, I want you to place Harland Castle and Pete Kendall under arrest and jail them. Formal charges will be laid within the hour.'

Buchanan's anger also flared from his eyes as he looked at the lawman still seated beside him. 'Sheriff Kendall, by the authority vested in me by the state of Colorado, I order you to hand over your badge, immediately.'

'Sure, Lawrence.' Kendall removed the badge from his shirt and tossed it onto the table. He stood up and using two fingers removed his gun from its holster and handed it to Emery Brown. Kendall then smiled in a wistful manner at the judge. 'Lawrence, I've been sheriff of Hard Stone for more than twenty years. Do you think that gives me some right to address the folks here before Emery marches me off?'

Buchanan's anger subsided a little. 'I reckon so. Keep it short.'

Pete Kendall faced the spectators. 'Nothing I say will make things right so I won't say much. But I want everyone to know this. Emery Brown had nothing to do with our crooked scheme. I guess most of you won't be in Hard Stone much longer, but while you are still here you can rely on Emery. He's one fine lawman.'

Embarrassed, Brown looked downwards. Moving his arm like a whip, Kendall grabbed the gun from Brown's holster and slammed it against his head. Kendall then pointed the gun at Dehner as the deputy crumbled to the floor.

'Don't move, Mr Detective, don't move!' Kendall hastily scooped up his own gun from the floor and pointed it in the direction of the spectators. 'Raise your hands, all of you! If I see anyone with his hands down, I'll shoot him and one other person!'

The spectators, who had already been shocked by the testimonies of the last two witnesses, followed Kendall's orders as they sat in a stunned silence. The former lawman made an intimidating figure as he stood before them, a gun in each hand.

Lawrence Buchanan sat at the judge's desk. He was now behind the disgraced sheriff. Buchanan started to move a hand toward his suit coat. Kendall swerved his left arm and flamed a bullet into the judge, who grabbed onto the arms of his chair, then plunged to the ground, the chair dropping on top of him.

Keeping his word, Pete Kendall streaked a second bullet into the body of an 11-year-old boy sitting in the second row. The boy gave a painful yell, stood up and took two steps before collapsing. His mother screamed as she ran to her son and crouched over him.

'That'll give the kid something to write about in his essay!' Madness filled Pete Kendall's eyes as a small group, including the town doctor, huddled around the wounded lad.

Kendall shouted a string of curses ending with, 'I wish I

had time to kill every one of you snakes.' He then ran out of the Lucky Miner.

For a moment, the crowd remained silent. The only sounds were the agonized cries of a distraught mother and the whispered babble of Judge Buchanan.

Shouts suddenly filled the room as the crowd threatened to become a mob. A few people ran to help Lawrence Buchanan while a few more joined the group already surrounding the wounded boy. Most people seemed to be heading nowhere as they yelled at each other in threatening voices.

Emery Brown was now on his feet and began to run after his former boss. Dehner stopped him.

'You're needed here.' Dehner had to shout for Brown to hear him over the bedlam. 'Try to calm this crowd, and get Harland Castle away from this place for his own protection. Lon and Stacey will help you.'

'But—'

'I'll go after Kendall!'

Brown reluctantly nodded his head. He moved quickly toward a group of angry people who were circling Harland Castle.

Dehner charged into the mass of humanity that swarmed between him and the Lucky Miner's batwings. The detective thought about firing his gun into the air to clear a path but decided against it. This mob perched on the edge of violence; a gunshot could push them over the precipice.

Outside on the boardwalk, Dehner noticed Emery Brown's claybank was no longer at the hitch rail in front of the saloon where he had seen him tie it a little more than an hour before. Kendall had most likely stolen it since the ex-lawman's horse was probably tethered in front of the sheriff's office and Kendall didn't want to expend the time needed to get it.

Dehner's bay was tethered at the hitch rail in front of the saloon. The detective regarded that as a touch of good luck, but he felt it wise not to count on having much more luck.

Dehner quickly untied his horse, mounted, and rode off after Pete Kendall.

CHAPTER TWENTY-SIX

Moments after galloping out of Hard Stone, Dehner spotted a dust cloud up ahead which could only be Pete Kendall. The detective kept his bay at a steady run but didn't push the animal.

He gained steadily on the disgraced lawman. As he approached a large hill with a flat top and steep slope that qualified it as a mesa, Dehner saw his adversary gracefully ride Brown's claybank up the steep slope. A smart move. Kendall had lived in Hard Stone for twenty years. He undoubtedly knew every cave and boulder on that mesa. He had a big advantage over Dehner.

Rance pulled up close to the hill but not too close. He needed to stay out of gun range. He had started to yank field glasses from one of his saddlebags when he heard hoofbeats prancing down the slope. Dehner forgot about the field glasses and palmed his Colt.

The claybank galloped off the slope and onto flat land. The horse was riderless. Pete Kendall was a man whose life had just come undone. He had been publicly humiliated and faced a jail sentence, possibly a rope. While riding a horse up a steep mesa he could have lost control of the animal and fallen off.

Dehner paused for a moment and took stock. *Yes, Kendall might have fallen off the horse but the claybank had run down the slope as if it had been slapped.*

The detective holstered his gun and slowly dismounted. He tied his bay to a nearby tree. The tree had plenty of leaves and the claybank began to clomp toward it. Dehner met the horse halfway. The boot on the claybank's saddle was empty.

Despite the circumstances, Dehner quietly chuckled. 'Nice try, Pete,' he whispered to himself. 'But you're not lying injured, you're lying in wait for me with Emery Brown's Henry ready for action.'

Dehner tied the claybank to the tree before pulling his Winchester from the boot of his own saddle. 'This case started with chasing a dangerous man up a steep slope.' The detective once again spoke to himself: 'Looks like it's going to end the same way.'

Dehner pulled his hat down low. He wanted his eyes covered to the extent it was possible. He started up the hill, pretending to be absorbed in following the trail which the claybank had left on its upward run.

The detective caught the sunlight glinting off the Henry in time to hit the ground and roll before Kendall fired. The shot burrowed into the earth scattering dirt as Dehner made it behind a boulder.

'Give it up, Kendall, you really don't want to kill me!'

'Hell, Dehner, the Pete Kendall you're talking 'bout is dead. I'm the Pete Kendall who just shot an old man and a kid. I'm as heartless as they come.'

Kendall was also sheltered behind a boulder, about fifteen yards up from the detective. Dehner laid down his rifle and pulled out his Colt. Though he didn't know exactly why, he wanted to keep his adversary talking. 'I guess you are heartless, Kendall. You and Snow planned to double-cross Harland Castle. Snow was never going to act confused over his testimony, was he?'

'You're right about that,' Kendall spoke loudly as he prepared to aim the Henry. 'Slushy and I wanted Westlake jailed for the robbery. It'd make ever' thing nice and neat. We thought the old man would have no choice but to go along. Ol' Harland surprised me today. I never thought the old coot would—'

Kendall fired the Henry. Dehner ducked down as stone chips fell on his neck. The detective heard sounds of running footsteps and loose gravel rolling down the mesa. He looked around the boulder and saw Pete Kendall running upwards.

The former lawman suddenly gave a loud yell of pain. He fell to the ground and rolled back behind the large stone that had provided him with cover. He frantically drew his pistol and sent a shot in Dehner's direction. The bullet, fired in panic, whistled harmlessly into the vast sky.

Kendall shouted several obscenities, which were almost as sharp and loud as the pistol shot. He then paused for a moment before calling out to his opponent. 'Know what's haywire 'bout this damn knee of mine, Dehner?'

Rance braced himself for another attack but still replied in a friendly voice from behind his cover. 'You were a sheriff. A lot of things could go wrong. Did you ever get shot in the leg?'

'Nothing like that! I've got arthritis. Been seeing the doc

'bout it for a year. Know what that no-good pill-pusher told me last time I saw him?'

Dehner listened carefully to Kendall's voice, which now sounded more desperate than angry. The detective kept his delivery casual and friendly. 'I never had much luck with sawbones myself. What did he say?'

'Said he expected me to be at the next town council meeting in September and hand in my resignation. The doc, of course, is one of the high and mighty members of the council.'

'And if you didn't resign he was going to tell the council about your arthritis and recommend they fire you.'

'The bastard! Twenty years of risking my life for Hard Stone and—'

'Was that about the time Harland came to you about the mine?'

'Yep. I saw a chance to grab a hold on some real money before leaving town for good. The only time in my life I went crooked and it turned out bad—real bad. Guess I didn't have enough practice.'

Dehner remembered one of his last conversations with Tully Brooks. The outlaw had stated that the one time he tried something decent he had ended up taking a bullet: a bullet that took his life hours later.

Once again Rance heard gravel rolling down toward him. This time, the footsteps were softer: Kendall was trying to sneak off.

Dehner took a cautious step to the side of his cover. Kendall was once again running toward the top of the mesa, this time with a limp.

The detective shouted, 'I'm giving you one last chance to surrender—'

Kendall turned and stumbled slightly. That stumble gave Dehner adequate time to jump back behind the boulder before Kendall fired the Henry at him.

'I ain't gonna spend the rest of my life in a jail cell, Dehner.'

Rance listened carefully to Kendall's footsteps as he climbed up the mesa. He waited a few moments, then holstered his .45. Winchester in hand, he slowly abandoned his cover and began to follow his adversary. But this time, he did not run. He walked steadily up the hill keeping the former lawman in sight.

Kendall was close to the top of the hill when he stopped, turned around, and saw Rance steadily moving toward him. 'Why don't you use that rifle of yours, Dehner? Maybe you can't hit a target from that far off!'

The disgraced lawman stood still for a moment watching Rance Dehner advance on him. The detective was now less than twenty yards away, but gave no indication of firing his Winchester or his Colt.

Kendall gave a loud laugh, then hobbled to the flat table top of the mesa. Dehner lost sight of him.

Rance slowed his advance but only slightly. At the top of the mesa were two boulders lying side by side. Both rocks only reached waist high. Pete would have to go down on his knees in order to get behind them.

Dehner listened for any sounds coming from the hilltop. But he really didn't have to listen carefully. Kendall was talking to himself in a tinny, high-pitched voice. 'Twenty years, twenty years, after twenty years you gotta quit. You're sick, you're no good, you're no good, you risked your life for twenty years, don't mean nothing now....'

Approaching the top of the mesa, Dehner folded into

a jackknife position. Reaching the boulders he remained head down as he laid his Winchester on the ground and palmed his Colt .45.

Kendall fired two shots into the air and then burst into maniacal laughter. Dehner peered over one of the boulders. Kendall was pacing back and forth, his pistol in one hand and the Henry in the other. Kendall continued to laugh but his eyes were moist with tears.

'Drop the guns, Kendall!' Dehner remained crouched as he pointed his Colt at the former lawman.

'Well, well, Rance! Looks like you get the honor of being the gent who kills Pete Kendall: Pete Kendall, that no-good snake who betrayed his badge!'

'I told you to drop the guns, Kendall.'

'Nope. You want my guns, you're gonna hafta kill me.'

'One last time, Kendall, drop the guns.'

This time Kendall's voice took on an air of mockery. 'One last time, Dehner, you're gonna have to kill me or I'll kill you!'

Kendall charged at Dehner firing his six-gun. As a bullet pinged off one of the boulders, Dehner did a quick duck walk to the far side of the boulders and squeezed off a shot, which cut into Kendall's shoulder.

Kendall stumbled sideways and continued to laugh as he turned and aimed at the detective. But one shot was all the former lawman would get. Dehner fired a red streak into Kendall's chest.

He now staggered backwards as he eyed the detective. He dropped the Henry first but held on to his pistol until he reached the edge of the mesa. He let go of the pistol as he closed his eyes and plunged downwards.

Dehner cautiously left his position and, Colt still in

hand, approached the place where Kendall had fallen. Still exercising caution he followed a red trail several feet down the mesa until he came to Pete Kendall's body, which was lying face down.

The detective lifted Kendall's wrist and felt for a pulse that wasn't there. Only then did Dehner holster his pistol.

He gazed upwards. The sky was a beautiful blend of blue and white. But Dehner didn't notice. He was seeing the expression on Pete Kendall's face. The look Kendall had given him as he realized the detective had killed him.

It was a look of gratitude.

CHAPTER TWENTY-SEVEN

For a second time, Rance Dehner rode into the town of Hard Stone leading a horse with a dead body draped over it. But this time people took an interest in the corpse. Pete Kendall was a man who only a few hours before had been their sheriff.

The atmosphere in Hard Stone was now much different than the day when Dehner had arrived with the body of Tully Brooks. The difference was exemplified by the buckboard in front of Westlake's General Store. The wagon stood packed with a few pieces of furniture and other personal belongings. Tom Flynn was helping the buckboard's owner to load on some supplies that had just been purchased for the trip from Hard Stone to … wherever there was work.

The town was already starting to die.

Fortunately, Henry Rimstead, the town's barber and

undertaker was still very much in business. After leaving the corpse of Pete Kendall with him, Dehner rode to the sheriff's office and tethered Emery Brown's claybank, as well as his own horse to the hitch rail in front.

Entering the office, Rance was surprised to see Stacey Hooper sitting at the sheriff's desk engaged in a game of solitaire. 'Welcome back, good friend,' Stacey looked up briefly from his cards. 'Will the former sheriff of Hard Stone be occupying one of the town's jail cells?'

'No. Pete Kendall is dead.'

'You killed him, I presume.'

'Yes. He forced me to kill him. He wanted to die.'

'Glad to know the man finally returned to his senses.'

'How are things here?'

Stacey's eyes were back on the cards. 'Following your hasty departure, I helped Emery Brown and the clergyman, Thorton Nevin, restore order and get Judge Buchanan and that kid to the doctor.'

'How are they doing?' Rance asked.

'How are who doing?'

'I'm talking about the judge and the boy!'

'Oh. I really can't say. Brown and the Nevin are running about looking after things right now. They should be able to bring you up when they return.'

'And while they are running about you are in charge of the office?'

Stacey beamed a smile at the detective: 'Only performing my civic duty.'

A few minutes later, Emery Brown and Thorton Nevin marched into the office looking tired and vaguely depressed, though they did have good news. Both Lawrence Buchanan and the boy would recover from the bullets Pete

Kendall had pumped into them.

'The kid will bounce back completely,' Brown explained. 'His Honor may lose some use of his left arm but he says that doesn't bother him. He can pound the gavel just fine with his right arm.'

That remark brought some faint smiles. Dehner asked: 'How is Harland Castle doing?'

Brown sighed and shook his head. 'I think Mr Castle hates himself. He gave me the cut of the money he received from the phony bank hold-up. He's home with his daughter and Lon right now. I'm giving Harland a little time to say his goodbyes in private, and then I'll have to arrest him and put him in jail. Hate to do it, but ....'

Thorton Nevin spoke as the deputy went silent. 'Penelope is deeply hurt and confused. She'll require a lot of time before she can forgive her father. I'll do what I can.'

'The preacher and I jawed some on our way back to the office,' Brown said. 'We both know Hard Stone is doomed. But a lot of folks in this town are angry and plenty upset. They need help. We're gonna stay here as long as we're needed. After that, I reckon I'll find another lawdog job somewhere.'

Reverend Nevin looked down at the floor and then faced his companions. 'And I'll find a town that needs to have a church built. A town that's willing to tolerate a pastor with a weak faith.'

'Don't be so hard on yourself, Preacher,' Brown immediately responded.

'A man needs to be honest about his failures.' Reverend Nevin spoke as if he were in a pulpit. 'I allowed an outlaw with a bare head and red ink on his face to convince me he was a man who had returned from the dead. I was convinced ghosts were everywhere. I thought I heard my brother speaking to my soul. And I'm supposed to be a man of faith! I won't hide my sins, but I won't let them stop me from doing good work, either. With the Lord's help, Tom and I will find a town where we can fit in.'

A quiet moment followed the pastor's declaration. Stacey Hooper broke the silence. 'Tell us, Rance, how did you figure Pete Kendall and Harland Castle as the main villains in this piece?'

'I did what I often do when I have no idea where to begin,' Dehner answered. 'I grab onto any detail that doesn't seem to quite fit.'

Stacey stood up and began to collect his cards, abandoning the game of solitaire. 'And, pray tell, exactly what was the minute detail that led to the collapse of a rather clever conspiracy?'

'On the night of the bank hold-up, Kendall and Emery Brown went to the home of Lon Westlake. Kendall ordered his deputy to confront Westlake while he checked the horse in the corral behind the house. That seemed a bit out of the ordinary. Usually, a sheriff will take the hardest job for himself.'

'I remember thinking the same thing at the time,' Emery Brown looked sheepish as he spoke. 'But I took it as sort of a compliment. My boss trusted me with the tough job. Guess I'm still pretty green.'

'Don't be so hard on yourself, Deputy.' Reverend Nevin smiled as he spoke.

Dehner continued: 'I checked with the hostler. The sheriff had brought Westlake's horse to the livery at the busiest time of his day. In other words, at a time when he would least remember what kind of condition the horse was in. Of course, Kendall was doing everything he could to cover the fact that the horse hadn't been ridden at all for a few days.'

Rance began to pace the office. 'Once I became suspicious of Pete Kendall, the whole puzzle began to come slowly together. I don't believe in spooks, so I took an interest in the fact that Kendall was the one who claimed Virgil Flynn's ghost left no tracks when he appeared outside the church. He ordered Reverend Nevin and Tom Flynn to stay inside. Of course, Kendall really destroyed the tracks left by the outlaw Willard Fanshaw.'

'Better known as Wild Willie,' Stacey added.

Reverend Nevin looked at Dehner intently as if recent events were beginning to make sense to him. 'And two people claimed Virgil Flynn's ghost left no tracks when he appeared at the window of the Castles' home: Pete Kendall and Harland Castle.'

The detective nodded his head. 'That is when my suspicions extended to Harland. His daughter didn't think to look for tracks. Once again, when the sheriff arrived he destroyed any trail Wild Willie had left.'

Emery Brown ran a hand across his forehead. 'If Harland and Kendall hadn't got so carried away with the ghost thing, their plan mighta worked.'

Stacey smiled approvingly at his friend, 'Tell us, Rance, were there any other little details you found to be of interest?'

'The situation with Slushy Snow didn't make much sense. Why would a mining engineer demand so much privacy for his work? And then there were those visitors you saw, Stacey, visitors who met a very nervous Slushy Snow in front of the saloon.'

'A most uncouth collection of villains,' Hooper added.

'But they never appeared again,' Dehner said. 'The explanation was obvious. Snow owed one of those men a lot of money. The jasper brought along some gunslicks to help him collect it. Slushy was able to pay him off and that was that.'

There was another quiet moment as men who had already absorbed a lot of bad news took in a bit more. This time, Dehner ended the quiet. 'You gents have a lot to do, so I won't take up much more of your time. I know an official of the Westward Bank of Commerce is now in town. I need to return the money we recovered to the bank and then I'll get out of your way.'

All four men in the office ended up accompanying Dehner to the bank, where most of the money was returned. The bank official seemed pleased, which meant Dehner's boss in Dallas would be pleased.

On the boardwalk outside the bank, Emery Brown and Reverend Nevin offered quick goodbyes to the detective. Like everyone else in Hard Stone, the two men had a lot to do and a lot of uncertainty in their lives. Dehner wished them well and asked them to say goodbye to Penelope Castle and Lon Westlake for him.

Stacey and Rance watched the two men head for the Castle home, where Harland would be arrested. Dehner questioned his friend as they walked back to the sheriff's office. 'What are your plans, Stacey?'

'I plan to remain in Hard Stone for a few days and be of help.'

'You're going to help Emery and the pastor?'

'Well … indirectly, yes. You see, there a lot of upset and desperate men in Hard Stone. These men need a way to safely blow off some steam, as the expression goes.'

'And you are going to help them get rid of all that steam by taking their money in poker games?'

'I will make one of their final nights in Hard Stone a night to remember. Meanwhile, I will rest my horse and see that he is properly cared for. A fast, late night exit from this town may well be in my immediate future.'

As they arrived in front of the sheriff's office, Dehner shook hands with the gambler. 'I would wish you good luck, Stacey, but somehow that seems unnecessary.'

Hooper laughed. 'Luck is for men who gamble and like I said, gambling is a sin.'

Dehner untied his bay, mounted, and gave Hooper a two-fingered salute. Stacey Hooper returned the gesture. 'I hope our paths cross again soon.'

Dehner shouted back, 'With my luck, they probably will.'

Later that evening, as he rode through mountainous country, Dehner thought about Harland Castle and Pete Kendall: good men who had worked hard and lived honestly and honorably until their lives collapsed and they could no longer be the men they once were.

Despite himself, Dehner felt guilty about Harland Castle. The detective had depended on Harland's basic goodness to help him solve the case. If Penelope's father hadn't confessed in court, Dehner would probably have been run out of town and the case never solved.

Yet, Harland Castle would almost certainly die in prison, his decades of living a fine, righteous life forgotten. Dehner remembered a quote from Shakespeare: *The evil that men do lives after them; the good is oft interred with their bones.*

Inevitably, the detective began to muse about the man

whom he had agreed to do a favor for, a man whose entire life had been spent on the wrong side of the law: Tully Brooks. A strange thought suddenly struck the detective. He would miss Tully Brooks. He would miss the excitement of trailing a clever outlaw who had tried to kill him and who he had eventually killed. A magnificent competition was now gone and the detective felt something meaningful had been taken from his own life.

The notion made Dehner give an involuntary guffaw. As the rocks around him echoed the laugh, a chilling wind blew between them. The warmth which had blanketed the area was in retreat. The night would be cold.